WANTING

From the international reviews:

'A beautifully constructed fugue on desire and its denial.'
TLS

'Light, mercurial... A novel of singular beauty and so vivid a
grace it inspires strange elation as well as pity for the lost.'
Irish Times

'Flanagan is a beautiful writer and *Wanting* is a beautiful and
considered addition to his oveuvre.' *The Age*

'*Wanting* is a novel you never want to end. As a reader, I can
offer no greater accolade.' *Canberra Times*

'In confident, expert hands, fiction can liberate the past...
Richard Flanagan is an exemplary case in point. Through
his fiction, flat, conformist portraits of individuals become
rich and three-dimensional, new witnesses provide fresh
testimony about the past, and Tasmania's silences resound
with voices... Mid-nineteenth-century London comes alive,
as indeed does Dickens himself.' William Boyd, *Scotsman*

'Moving seamlessly through time, across two continents and between three storylines, *Wanting* is a marvel of precision and cohesion... Flanagan knows even the strongest yearning can mean nothing against the tides of fate. His beautifully bleak riffs on this universal theme make *Wanting* one of the finest novels of the year.' *Sun-Herald* (Sydney)

'An exquisite, profoundly moving, intricately structured meditation about the desire for human connection.' *Los Angeles Times*

'Dazzling... A captivating tale of cruelty and disappointment.' *Washington Post*

'Flanagan forges an entirely unified meditation on desire, "the cost of its denial, the centrality and force of its power in human affairs."' *New Yorker*

'Haunting and powerful... Flanagan does a magical job of conjuring his native Tasmania as it must have appeared to English settlers.' *New York Times*

'Flanagan's meditation on its ramifications, his careful weaving of history and fiction, and his hard gaze at human behaviour make clear that want is central to human life... His book is stark and affecting... hard to forget.' *Washington Times*

RICHARD FLANAGAN

WANTING

Atlantic Books
LONDON

First published in Australia in 2008 by Random House Australia Pty Ltd,
Level 3, 100 Pacific Highway, North Sydney, NSW 2060.

First published in hardback and export and airside trade
paperback in Great Britain in 2009 by Atlantic Books, an imprint
of Grove Atlantic Ltd.

This paperback edition published in Great Britain
in 2010 by Atlantic Books.

Epigraph from *Notes from Underground* by Fyodor Dostoevsky,
translated by Richard Pevear and Larissa Volokhonsky, published by Vintage.
Reprinted by permission of The Random House Group Ltd.

Typeset and designed by Midland Typesetters, Australia.

1 3 5 7 9 10 8 6 4 2

A CIP catalogue record for this book is available from the
British Library.

ISBN: 978 1 84887 077 2

Printed in Great Britain by CPI Bookmarque, Croydon

Atlantic Books
An imprint of Grove Atlantic Ltd
Ormond House
26–27 Boswell Street
London
WC1N 3JZ

www.atlantic-books.co.uk

For Kevin Perkins

You see, reason, gentlemen, is a fine thing, that is unquestionable, but reason is only reason and satisfies only man's reasoning capacity, while wanting is a manifestation of the whole of life.

Fyodor Dostoevsky

That which is wanting cannot be numbered.

Ecclesiastes

WANTING

I

THE WAR HAD ENDED as wars sometimes do, unexpectedly. A man no one much cared for, a rather pumped-up little Presbyterian carpenter cum preacher, had travelled unarmed and in the company of tame blacks through the great wild lands of the island, and had returned with a motley cluster of savages. They were called wild blacks, though wild they most certainly were not, but rather scabby, miserable and often consumptive. They were, he said—and remarkably it did now seem—all that remained of the once feared Van Diemonian tribes that for so long had waged relentless and terrible war.

Those who saw them said it was hard to believe that such a small and wretched bunch could have defied the might of the Empire for so long, that they could have survived the pitiless extermination, that they could have been the instruments of such fear and terror. It wasn't clear what the preacher had said to the blacks, or what the blacks thought he was going to do with them, but they seemed amenable, if somewhat sad, as broken party after broken party were embarked on boat after boat and taken to a distant island that lay in the hundreds of miles of sea that separated Van Diemen's Land from the Australian mainland. Here the preacher took on the official title of Protector and a salary of £500 a year, along with a small garrison of soldiers and a Catechist, and set about raising his sable charges to the level of English civilisation.

He met with some successes, and, though these were small, it was on such he tried to concentrate. And were they not worthy? Were his people not knowledgeable of God and Jesus, as was evidenced by their ready and keen answers to the Catechist's questions, and evinced in their enthusiastic hymn-singing? Did they not take keenly to the weekly market, where they traded skins and shell necklaces for beads and tobacco and the like? Other than that his black brethren kept dying almost daily, it had to be admitted the settlement was satisfactory in every way.

Some things, however, were frankly perplexing. Though he was weaning them off their native diet of berries and plants and shellfish and game, and onto flour and sugar and tea, their health seemed in no way comparable to what it had been. And the more they took to English blankets and heavy English clothes, abandoning their licentious nakedness, the more they coughed and spluttered and died. And the more they died, the more they wanted to cast off their English clothes and stop eating their English food and move out of their English homes, which they said were filled with the Devil, and return to the pleasures of the hunt of a day and the open fire of a night.

It was 1839. The first photograph of a man was taken, Abd al-Qadir declared a jihad against the French, and Charles Dickens was rising to greater fame with a novel called *Oliver Twist*. It was, thought the Protector as he closed the ledger after another post mortem report and returned to preparing notes for his pneumatics lecture, inexplicable.

2

ON HEARING THE NEWS of the child's death from a servant who had rushed from Charles Dickens' home, John Forster had not hesitated—hesitation was a sign of a failure of character, and his own character did not permit failure. Mastiff-faced, full-bodied and goose-bellied, heavy in all things—opinion, sensibility, morality and conversation—Forster was to Dickens as gravity to a balloonist. Though not above mimicking him in private, Dickens was immensely fond of his unofficial secretary, on whom he relied for all manner of work and advice.

And Forster, inordinately proud of being so relied on, decided he would wait until Dickens had given his speech. In spite of Forster's ongoing arguments that recent events excused Dickens from the necessity of addressing the General Theatrical Fund, he had been unwavering that he would. Why, even that very day Forster had called on

Dickens at Devonshire Terrace to urge him one last time to cancel the engagement.

'But I've promised,' said Dickens, whom Forster had found in the garden playing with his younger children. He had in his arms his ninth child, the baby Dora, and he'd lifted her above his head, smiling up at her and blowing through his lips as she beat her arms up and down, fierce and solemn as a regimental drummer. 'No, no; I could not let us down like that.'

Forster had swelled, but said nothing. Us! He knew Dickens sometimes thought of himself more as an actor than a writer. It was a nonsense, but it was him. Dickens loved theatre. He loved everything to do with that world of make-believe, where the moon might be summoned down with a flourish of a finger, and Forster knew Dickens felt a strange solidarity with the actor members of the troupers' charity, which he was to address that evening. This attraction to the more disreputable both slightly troubled and slightly thrilled Forster.

'She looks well, don't you think?' Dickens had said, lowering the baby to his chest. 'She's had a slight fever today, haven't you, Dora?' He kissed her forehead. 'But I think she's picking up now.'

And now, only a few short hours later, how splendidly Dickens' speech was going, thought Forster. The crowd was extensive, its attention rapt, and Dickens, once started, as brilliant and moving as ever.

'In our Fund,' Dickens was saying to the crowded hall of actors, 'the word exclusiveness is not known. We include every actor, whether he is Hamlet or Benedict: this ghost, that bandit, or, in his one person, the whole King's army. And to play their parts before us, these actors come from scenes of sickness, of suffering, aye, even of death itself. Yet—'

There was a stuttering of applause that stopped almost before it started, perhaps because it was felt bad taste to draw attention to Dickens' being there just two weeks after his own father's death. A failed operation for bladder stones had left the old man, Dickens had told Forster, lying in a slaughterhouse of blood.

'Yet how often it is,' continued Dickens, 'that we have to do violence to our feelings, and hide our hearts in carrying on this fight of life, so we can bravely discharge our duties and responsibilities.'

After, Forster took Dickens aside.

'I am afraid . . .' Forster began. 'In a word,' said Forster, who always used too many, but now realised there was one he did not wish to utter.

'Yes?' said Dickens, eyeing somebody or something over Forster's shoulder, then looking back, eyes twinkling. 'Yes, my dear Mammoth?'

His casual use of Forster's nickname, his presumption all this was just banter, the pleasure of the performer at the success of a performance—none of it helped make poor Forster's task any easier.

'Little Dora . . .' said Forster. His lips twitched as he tried to finish the sentence.

'Dora?'

'I am,' mumbled Forster, wishing at that moment to say so many things, but unable to say any of them. 'I am, so, so sorry, Charles,' he said in a rush, regretting every word, wanting something so much better to say, his hand rising to emphasise with its customary flourish some point never made, then falling back to the side of his body, his big body that felt so bloated and useless. 'She was taken with convulsions,' he said finally.

Dickens' face showed no emotion, and Forster thought what a splendid man he was.

'When?' asked Dickens.

'Three hours ago,' said Forster. 'Just after we left.'

It was 1851. London's Great Exhibition celebrated the triumph of reason in a glass pavilion mocked by the writer Douglas Jerrold as a crystal palace; a novel about finding a fabled white whale was published in New York to failure; while in the iron-grey port of Stromness, Orkney, Lady Jane Franklin farewelled into whiteness the second of what were to be numerous failed expeditions in search of a fable that had once been her husband.

3

A SMALL GIRL RAN FIT TO BURST through wallaby grass
almost as high as her. How she loved the sensation of the
soft threads of fine grass feathering beads of water onto her
calves, and the feel of the earth beneath her bare feet, wet
and mushy in winter, dry and dusty in summer. She was
seven years old, the earth was still new and extraordinary
in its delights, the earth still ran up through her feet to her
head into the sun, and it was as possible to be exhilarated
by running as it was to be terrified by the reason she had to
run and not stop running. She knew stories of spirits who
could fly and wondered whether, if she ran that little bit
faster, she might also fly and reach her destination quicker.
Then she remembered that only the dead flew and put all
thought of flying out of her mind.

She ran past the homes in which the blackfellas lived,
she ran through chooks clacking and dogs barking, past the

chapel, and she kept running, up the slope of the hill to the most important building in the settlement of Wybalenna. She climbed its three steps and, as she had been shown again and again, hit the door in the whitefella way with a bunched hand.

The Protector looked up from his pneumatics lecture notes to see a small native girl enter the house. She was barefoot in a filthy pinafore and a red woollen stocking hat, and a candledrip of snot leapt in and out of her right nostril like a living thing. She looked up at the ceiling and she looked around the walls. Mostly she looked at the floor.

'Yes?' said the Protector. In the irritating way of her people, she looked everywhere but in his eyes. Her real name was the one he had christened her with, Leda, but for some reason everyone else called her by her native name. He was annoyed to find himself now doing the same. 'Yes, Mathinna?'

Mathinna looked at her feet, scratched under an arm. But she didn't say anything.

'Well, what is it? What, child?'

And suddenly realising why she was there, Mathinna said, 'Rowra,' using the native word for the Devil, then quickly, like it was a spear rushing at her, '*Rowra*,' and then 'ROWRA!'

The Protector jumped off his stool, grabbed a folding knife from an open drawer and ran outside, the child making haste before him. They ran to a row of conjoined brick terraces he had built for the natives, to accustom them to English domesticity and to break them away from their own rude windbreaks. It ever pleased the Protector, who had been a carpenter before he became a saviour, how—if one didn't think of the white beach behind, red-bouldered and leathery kelp-rimed, or the woodlands beyond, strange and twisted; if one just ignored this wretched wild island on which they sat at the edge of the world and instead concentrated on these buildings— it was possible to see that the two rows of tenements looked for all the world like some newly built street in a great modern town like Manchester.

As they approached house number 17, Mathinna halted for a moment, stared at the sky above, and seemed transfixed by some nameless terror. The Protector was about to rush past her when he saw the omen the natives feared the most, the bird that stole souls, a black swan swooping down towards the brick terraces.

Even before he was inside, the Protector was beset by a strong odour of muttonbird grease, unwashed bodies and a fear—wordless, nameless—that somehow this rotting stench related to him, to his actions, his beliefs. Sometimes the idea would come into his mind that these people he loved so much, whom he had protected from the depredations of the cruellest white settlers—who hunted them down and shot them with as much glee as they hunted kangaroo, and with as little care—that these people whom he had brought to God's light were yet dying in some strange way, in consequence of him. He knew it was an irrational idea. A perverse, impossible idea. He knew that it came from weariness. But he could not stop the idea returning again and again. At such times he often felt headaches come on, intense pains at the front of his head so wretched he had to take to his bed.

In the post mortems he searched their split oesophagi, their disembowelled bellies, their pus-raddled intestines and shrivelled lungs for some evidence of his guilt or innocence, but he could find none. He tried to embrace as penance the stench of the pints of pus that sometimes seemed the only life force in their wretched guts. He tried to understand their suffering as his, and the day he vomited from the sight of bright mould an inch thick rising like a crop around a crater-like ulcer that ran from Black Ajax's armpit almost to his hip, he tried to see it as some necessary reckoning of a spiritual ledger. But puking was no reckoning, and in his heart the Protector feared there could be none. In his heart he feared that this ferocious suffering, these monstrous deaths, were all in consequence of him.

He did all he could do to save them in such circumstances—God knew he could not have done more—carefully cutting up each body to try to find the cause of death, getting up in the middle of the night and cupping and leeching and blistering and, as he was about to do now to Mathinna's father, bleeding.

The Protector opened his folding knife, wet his index finger and thumb, and ran them along the blade to clean it of the blood crust that was now all that remained above this earth of Wheezy Tom. He cut the shuddering man's wrist carefully, scientifically, shallowly, at the point where maximum blood could be released with minimum damage.

When by candlelight each night before bed he made up his journal entry, the Protector searched for words that might be made to fit, as in another life he had made timber bend and warp to fit. He searched for a length of words that, like a batten, might act as a covering strip for some inexplicable yet shameful error. But words only amplified the darkness he felt; covered it but could not explain it. At such times he reached for prayer, hymn, familiar patterns, reassuring rhythms. And sometimes these holy words held it all at bay, and he knew why he was grateful to God, and also why he feared Him.

Blood spurted up in a small geyser, hitting the Protector in the eye then running down his face. He pulled the knife away, then stepped back, wiped his eye and looked down. The emaciated black man was groaning only intermittently now. The Protector admired his stoicism: he took to bleeding like a white man.

It was King Romeo, a man once vital and friendly, a man—*the* man—who had swum into the Fury River and rescued him, the Protector, when he had lost his footing trying to ford the rising waters. Yet in the wretched, sunken features, in the unnaturally large eyes, the lank hair, he could recognise nothing of that man.

He let the blood pump for a good minute, catching it as best he could in a large pannikin. As it surged, King

Romeo made a low moaning noise. The black women seated on the floor in a crescent around his cot made a similar dirge at the back of their throats and the Protector knew they were much affected.

As he bound King Romeo's wound to stem the flow, the Protector sensed the inevitability of death and the futility of his treatment, and he felt a panic take hold of him. He realised King Romeo was breathing heavily, that the bleeding was pointless, that he had wished to hurt the black man for his incurable illness, for all their incurable illnesses, for all their failures to allow him to cure them, to civilise them, to give them the chance no one else cared to give them.

Muttering something about the necessity of equalising pneumatic forces within and without—to reassure himself as much as to impress upon his audience that his actions were, as ever, guided by a correct mix of rational science and Christian compassion—the Protector roughly seized King Romeo's other arm. The black man cried out in pain as, this time, he more stabbed than cut his arm.

He let King Romeo bleed till his patient's skin was clammy and the Protector once more felt calm. Then he staunched the flow and handed the brimming pannikin of blood to one of the crescent of black women, indicating she was to dispose of it outside.

The Protector straightened up, bowed his head and began to sing.

'*Lead, kindly Light, amid th' encircling gloom; lead Thou me on!*'

His voice was quavering and shrill. He swallowed, then with a deeper, louder and more determined baritone continued.

'*The night is dark, and I am far from home; lead Thou me on!*'

The black women seemed to be joining in—badly, it was true—but then he realised that they had merely altered their dirge-like keening to meld with his hymn.

'*Remember not past years!*' he sang, now at the top of his voice, but sometimes even he could not erase the past years. He halted mid-verse but they did not. He rolled his sleeves back down, turned around and was surprised to see Mathinna looking intently at him, as though at once believing he had magical powers and seeking to divine what they were, and yet beginning to doubt the sorcerer's potency. Unsettled, he searched for a new rhythm of words to soothe his nerves.

'Now is the period in which King Romeo's pulmonary system will find its equilibrium,' the Protector began. 'Whereby well-being . . . such that blood . . .'

Mathinna looked down at her naked feet, and so too for a moment did the Protector; then, feeling an embarrassment verging on inexplicable shame, he looked back up and away, and walked out of the hut into the relief of the cold sea air.

He felt angry, but his anger perplexed him. This was the surgeon's work, but the surgeon had himself died miserably a month before, and his replacement was promised but could yet be months away. And as angry as he was with the old surgeon for succumbing to dysentery, furious as he was with the Governor for not replacing him more speedily, he was proud of his own ability as a man of medicine, a man who knew how to bleed and blister, who could prepare enemas and dissect corpses and write competent reports—he, a layman, a carpenter, self-reliant and self-made and self-taught, the very triumph of self.

In the afternoon the Protector spent his time to achieve what he felt was good profit, preparing plans for a new, larger cemetery to cope with the mortality that was afflicting the settlement. Near dusk he went to the old burial ground with the natives and asked them to tell him the names of the buried. They seemed very apprehensive to name any of the dead, and, disgruntled at such ingratitude, he dismissed them.

The Protector was determined his new burial ground be complete for the imminent visit of the Van Diemonian Governor, Sir John Franklin, and his wife, Lady Jane, expected a week hence. The wind was gusting up from the south: with such favourable weather it could well be earlier. Sir John was a man of science, one of the age's greatest explorers and a man of many projects, whether they be exploring the vast Transylvanian wilds of the island's west or founding scientific societies or collecting shells and flowers for Kew Gardens.

Yes, thought the Protector as he paced out the exact dimensions of the graveyard, a new cemetery and a raising of the standards of the natives' hymn-singing were real and reasonable goals that he could achieve before the vice-regal visit. Above all else, the Protector prided himself on his realism.

That evening the Protector gave his lecture on pneumatics to an audience that combined the officers and their families and the natives. His final text ran to one hundred and forty-four pages. He felt he had well advanced his argument with logic and occasional practical example, such as when he heated a bottle over a steaming kettle he had hanging over the fire. By holding the bottle over a peeled boiled egg, the egg was slowly sucked up into the bottle.

Troilus laughed at this point and said loudly, 'Wybalenna bottle, blackfella egg,' drawing entirely the wrong principle from the demonstration.

After, the Protector shared a glass of hock and some ham sandwiches with the officers, and to show he would tolerate no distinction between black and white, also partook of a pannikin of tea that was served to the natives, which he felt they relished.

King Romeo was found dead the following morning. In truth, his passing was neither unexpected nor unfamiliar, and when the Protector went to examine the body, he felt boredom possessing him in the way pity once had. A woman with whom King Romeo had taken up after the death of his wife a few years earlier was in the normal state of native overexcitement, wailing like a belfry being rung by a madman, her face so many trails of blood from where she had purposely cut herself with a piece of broken bottle.

King Romeo's daughter, however, seemed possessed of a more Christian sensibility and in her demure grief afforded the Protector some hope that his work was something more than the most colossal vanity. The child was so quiet he wondered if perhaps she might be more amenable to a civilising influence than he had previously thought.

In consequence of attending to King Romeo's corpse, he was late for the school of which he was master, a failure of punctuality that made the Protector angry with the dead man: example, after all, was everything. If his own example was in any way lacking, how could he expect the natives to change their ways?

His lateness was misread by those in attendance as a loosening of discipline; they continued talking and laughing even while he spoke to them. He found himself furious with them, and rather than beginning the day with the catechism, he berated his class. Had he ever deceived them? Had he not provided good, warm and substantial new brick dwellings? Good raiment? Food in abundance? Moreover, had he not determined to reorganise their dead and put marks above each grave so they might know who was buried where?

After a light lunch of several muttonbirds and bread, he went to the hut that was kept for surgery and post mortems. On a long pine table within lay the body of King Romeo. Later he entered the results of his work as follows:

*Died of a general decay of nature: lung adhered to the chest
so firmly that it required force to separate it; chest contained
large amount of fluid: morbid lung and the spleen and
the urethra and appendages were taken out and are to be
conveyed to Hobarton for the inspection of dr arthur: he were
an interesting man.*

At the autopsy's end, the Protector took out of a
wooden case a meat saw he kept specially sharpened and
reserved for one purpose only. He favoured it because its
ebony handle was heavily crosshatched, allowing him to
maintain a firm grip even once his hand was wet, thereby
ensuring the neatest job.

He was about to begin when there was a knock on the
door, and he opened it to see the native woman Aphrodite
begging him to come to her house: her husband, Troilus,
was having fits. The Protector spoke to her in his gentlest
voice. A voice of pity, he felt. He told her to return to her
husband, that he would come soon to minister to him. He
closed the door. He returned to the corpse. He placed the
saw's edge precisely in the nape of the neck.

Had he become God? He no longer knew. They kept
dying. He was surrounded by corpses, skulls, autopsy
reports, plans for the chapel and cemetery. His dreams
were full of their dances and songs, the beauty of their
villages, the sound of their rivers, the memory of their
tendernesses, yet still they kept dying and nothing he did
altered it. They kept dying and dying, and he—who had
lived in their old world, who continued to work to make

this new world perfect in its civilisation, its Christianity, its Englishness—he was their Protector, but still they kept dying. If he was God, what god was he?

He drew the saw carefully across the skin to score a red guiding line. Then, good tradesman that he was, he completed the job with long, firm strokes, counting them as he went. It took just six to saw off King Romeo's head. Careful as the Protector was, he was annoyed to feel his hands greasy with blood.

4

AS IT HAPPENED, it was said he had rather gone off the boil. Lord Macaulay had told her the man's latest novel was little more than sullen socialism, its plot implausible and the whole ruined by his cheap pamphleteering. She had not read it, preferring the classics to entertainments. He was no immortal like Thackeray.

Looking up at him as she picked up the teapot and leaned forward, Lady Jane Franklin saw a small man who seemed worn beyond his middle years. Though he still wore his hair in a dandyish long cut, it was thinning and greying, framing a gaunt, furrowed face. She wondered if the real question were not whether his books would survive him, but whether he would much longer survive his books. Still, while alive, he remained the most popular writer in the land. While he lived, his opinion could move governments. And as long as he continued to draw breath, he was the best ally she could hope to make.

'More tea?' she asked.

He accepted with a smile. She ignored the stubby fingers holding out the saucer and cup—more befitting, she felt, of a navvy than a novelist—just as she ignored the overly bright clothing, the excess of jewellery, the way he seemed to be devouring her just as he had the poppyseed cake, all in a greedy rush, leaving on his lips a jetsam of yellow crumbs and black seeds. He put her in mind of a shrivelling hermit crab staring out of its gaudy shell. It all might almost have been disagreeable, were it not for who he most certainly was. That she did not ignore.

'Milk, Mr Dickens?'

And so that wintry morning in London she told him her story, burnished bright and honed sharp by countless telling, of the expedition, a task only the English in their greatness would even dare contemplate: to go where none had ever been; to discover at the very edge of the world the route of which men had for centuries only dreamt, the fabled Northwest Passage through the Arctic ice.

Though Dickens knew much of it—who did not?—he listened patiently. Lady Jane spoke of the two splendid ships, the *Terror* and the *Erebus*, returned from their epic Antarctic voyage and fitted out with the most modern engineering marvels: steam engines and retractable screw propellers, copper sheathing, steam heating, even a steam-powered organ that could automatically play popular tunes. By virtue of a remarkable new invention, they carried an abundance of food preserved in thousands of tin-plate canisters. And she made all this detail of the expedition—the most expensive, most remarkable ever to be sent out by the Royal Navy—fascinating, even compelling.

But it was on the calibre of the officers and crew that she dwelt—the very finest of Englishmen, including the remarkable veteran of the southern polar exploration, Captain Crozier, and finally its leader, her husband, Sir John Franklin: his indomitable character, his gentle but inexorable will, his remarkable capacity for leadership, his extraordinary and heroic contribution to Arctic exploration, his embodiment of all that was most virtuous in English civilisation. But nothing had been heard of him or his one hundred and twenty-nine men since they sailed for the northern polar regions nine years before.

'Is it any wonder, then, that this mystery has captured the imagination of the civilised world?' said Lady Jane, trying not to be distracted by the sound of Dickens sucking his tongue in odd concentration. 'For how is it possible for so many so remarkable to vanish off the face of the earth for so long without trace?'

Sitting there, he had a vision that would become inescapable, at once a talisman, a mystery, an explanation and a lodestone—the frozen ship, leaning on some unnatural angle, forced upwards and sideways by the ice, immense white walls rearing behind its dipping masts, the glitter of moonlight on endless snow, the desolate sound of men moaning as they died echoing across the infinite expanse of windswept white. In its strange hallucinatory power, Dickens had the odd sensation of recognising himself as ice floes, falling snow, as if he were an infinite frozen world waiting for an impossible redemption.

'Greatness like Sir John's comes but once in an age,' he said, seeking to wrench his fancy free from these terrible visions. 'A Magellan, a Columbus, a Franklin—they do not vanish, neither from the earth nor from history.'

Lady Jane Franklin had extensive acquaintances, bad breath, and was dreaded in more than one circle. There was no accounting for her triumphs. It was said that she was a woman of beguiling charm, but looking at her that morning, Dickens could see little of it. Rather than the black of a widow's weeds, she wore a green and purple dress, down the front of which hung a bright pendant showing Sir John in white Wedgwood profile—an odd touch, Dickens felt. It was as if Sir John were already an ice man.

'What with all that bunting, she was more a semaphore station than a Lady of the Realm,' he later told his friend Wilkie Collins, 'signalling the Lords of the Admiralty and the Ladies of Society one thing and one thing only: *My husband is not dead!* Is it gaudy or godly,' he added, 'to pronounce one's marital loyalty so?'

Still, none seemed immune to her message—how could he deny it? She spoke of her personal communications with the highest, not only in England but around the world. Everyone from the Muscovy Czar to American railroad millionaires had sent out rescue missions, and every mission had returned with nothing.

Yet Lady Jane maintained her determined love, her refusal to accept a mystery as a tragedy. Nothing had elevated a woman higher in the eyes of the English public than her refusal to sink with grief. And though her husband had left nine years before—with three years of food and almost as much fanfare—the English public, ever pleased, as Dickens well knew, with the possibility of outrageous coincidence, agreed that she was right; the English public was certain that there was no reason *at all* to suggest that Sir John—a great Englishman in the stoutest English company ever assembled for such a venture—would not endure where even savages could survive.

'And now this,' Lady Jane said, her voice suddenly Arctic ice itself, taking from a side table a folded newspaper and passing it to Dickens. 'I'm sure you've read it.'

He hadn't. But of course he had heard of it. It was *The Illustrated London News*, and one article bore numerous green ink markings. It was an account by a noted Arctic explorer, Dr John Rae, of the remarkable and gruesome discoveries he had made in the farthest polar reaches. The dreadful news had flown around London, amazed Europe and stunned the Empire.

It appeared a terrible possibility, Lady Jane went on, from Dr Rae's evidence, and from the more incontrovertible assembly of relics he had brought back—broken watches, compasses, telescopes, a surgeon's knife, an order of merit, several silver forks and spoons with the Franklin crest, and a small silver plate engraved 'Sir John Franklin, K. C. H.'—that all of the expedition had most tragically perished. She had to admit to the possibility. She did not deny it—but it remained, until irrefutable evidence emerged, *only* a possibility.

As an old newspaperman, Dickens found newspapers an ever less satisfactory form of fiction. He skimmed the opening columns. They recounted how, after much adventuring, Dr Rae had met with Esquimaux who possessed bric-a-brac clearly from Franklin's expedition; after numerous careful interviews, Rae had put together a chilling tale. Dickens' eyes halted at a passage down the side of which ran a long wavering green line. It was the only passage he read properly.

'But this,' said Lady Jane finally, 'is not a possibility. This is unbearable.'

It was astonishing.

'*From the mutilated state of many of the bodies and the contents of the kettles,*' Dickens read a second time, admiring the marvellous detail of the kettles, '*it is evident that our wretched Countrymen had been driven to the last dread alternative—cannibalism—as a means of prolonging existence.*'

'It is a lie,' said Lady Jane. 'A nonsense. And its sensational airing is an insult to the memory of these greatest of Englishmen.'

Handing the newspaper back, Dickens studied her face closely.

'If my husband has perished, he has none but me left to save his honour from such slander. If he is alive, then how is it possible to ask either the great or the many for further help to find him if Dr Rae's view prevails?'

And now, for the first time, Dickens understood that her sole purpose was to seek his help in damning Dr Rae and his account. Lady Jane wanted him to put an end to these dreadful rumours of Sir John eating his fellows. Well, thought Dickens as he continued to listen solemnly, he would have to eat *something* to maintain that enormous bulk of his.

'You see, Mr Dickens, the question that arises?'

'I do see, Lady Jane.'

And he did. This famous woman wanted his help. He, who had known such shame as the son of a man imprisoned for debt; he, a one-time bootblack labeller, a scribbler and chancer got lucky. He had made of himself something, indeed everything; and here, in Lady Jane's every word, he had undeniable proof of it: a celebrated Lady of the Realm wanting from him what even the powerful did not seem to possess. He, the debtor's son, was now to be the creditor.

'Can such testimony be trusted?' she asked.

'Can rat cunning ever be called truthful witness?'

'Indeed,' said Lady Jane, momentarily startled. 'That's precisely it.' She halted, lost in some distant, elusive thought, then spoke as if reciting something learnt long ago by painful rote. '*Rats*, we know, have cunning,' she said slowly, 'but we do not think such cunning equates with humanity or civilisation. While they are rewarded, they pretend to one thing. Yet they are capable of the grossest deceit of . . .'

Lady Jane was falling into some unexpectedly deep feeling that for a moment made her stammer. Mistaking this as grief for her husband, Dickens was touched by what was clearly a more genuine emotion than she had hitherto shown. He had found something unearthly, even ridiculous, in her triumphant rendering of her husband. Part of him despised such nonsense. But another part of him wanted to share in it, to shore up its leaking holes, to buttress and burnish this improbable story of English greatness and English goodness.

'I did what I . . .' she began, but then for an instant she thought somebody, something was tugging at her skirts. She twisted around in her seat, expecting to see a small girl in a red dress. But there was no one. A friend had written some years before from Van Diemen's Land telling her what had become of Mathinna.

Lady Jane longed to stand up, run away; wished for someone, anyone, to wash and soothe her, comfort her. She wished to be held. She wished to feel her dress being tugged. She saw red garments unloose parrots, possums, snakes. When she was young, she had wanted to be known as sweet. She was not sweet. She had fallen such a long way. She remembered the softness of those dark eyes; the sight that once had angered her and now moved her so, of those bare feet.

'Their destiny,' her correspondent had concluded, 'can only be interrupted by kindness, but never altered by it.'

I am so alone, she thought. Those bare, black feet. She had burnt the letter and then done something uncharacteristic. She had cried.

She looked up. Her head steadied her reckless heart

which had once, long ago, caused her such trouble. Though she feared the great novelist might find her aged and vile, she wanted her words to accord with common sense.

'I have had experience of such people,' said Lady Jane finally, and her voice oddly hardened. 'Not the Esquimaux, but similar savages. The Van Diemonians—'

'Cannibals?' Dickens interrupted.

Lady Jane remembered her last sight of the bedraggled child, alone in the muddy squalor of that courtyard. She felt gripped by pain, as if in a terrible retribution she only dimly apprehended, as though it were a vengeance that might consume her completely as the ice had her husband. She forced herself once more to smile.

'Your husband,' said Dickens. 'I cannot begin to compass your terrible—'

'No,' she said. 'Not that I . . .' She paused. She thought she smelt damp sandstone. 'It is difficult,' she went on—but what was she saying? Still she went on, trying to fashion belief and certainty out of words that felt comfortable. 'It is impossible to form an estimate of the character of any race of savages from the way they defer to the white man when he is strong.'

'I beg to say,' said Dickens, smiling, 'that I have not the least belief in the noble savage.'

'Of course, such things are not unknown, even to white men. After all, in Van Diemen's Land there were cases of escaping convicts taking vile resort in eating each other. But they were men devoid of religion, a hundred times

29

worse than the most barbarous heathens because they had turned away. You see, Mr Dickens, the distance between savagery and civilisation is—'

But had she not said such things before? Something seemed wrong—with her reasoning, or her memory, or how she had once behaved. Just when she felt uncharacteristically faint and lost, Dickens rescued her.

'The distance, Ma'am, is the extent we advance from desire to reason.' He would not tell her his whole life was an object lesson in control of one's passions; that it was what had led him to sit there with her that very day.

'I do not entirely agree with those that say it is a matter of science,' said Lady Jane. 'Rather it is an affair of the spirit.'

She stood up and went to a display cabinet, from which she took a wooden box. Sitting it on the mahogany *guéridon* between her and Dickens, she raised the lid. Inside, cushioned by red felt, were a few folded letters and a yellowing skull.

'It is a king of the Van Diemonian savages, Mr Dickens. I have shown it to several professors and men learned in phrenology. To test them, I did not say who it once was. Some found irrefutable signs in the skull's shape of degeneracy, others of nobility. It appears it is both.'

'The convict, the Esquimau, the savage: all are enslaved not by the bone around their brain,' said Dickens, reaching across and closing the lid, 'but by their passions.' He raised his hand with a flourish, as he did when performing. 'A man like Sir John is liberated from such by his civilised and Christian spirit.'

'Exactly,' said Lady Jane.

'As for the noble savage, I call him an enormous nuisance and I don't care what he calls me. It is all one to me whether he boils his brother in a kettle or dresses as a seal. He can yield to whatever passion he wishes, but for that very reason, he is a savage—a bloodthirsty wild animal whose principal amusement comes from stories at best ridiculous and at worst lies.'

'Lies, you say, Mr Dickens?'

'I do say, Lady Jane. Terrible, wretched, disgusting, mirroring lies. Here we have a race of thieving, murdering cannibals asserting that England's finest were transformed into thieving, murdering cannibals—what remarkable coincidence!'

'They had evidence, Mr Dickens,' said Lady Jane.

'Murderous thieves produce damning evidence of murderous thievery—and what do we do?' said Dickens, picking up *The Illustrated London News*. He waved it as a parliamentarian would a deficient bill, his triumphant smile perfectly judged. 'Broadcast their story of innocence, that's what!'

Later, when he came to kiss her liver-spotted hand in farewell, Lady Jane asked him if it was in his power to question such a story.

'I only know I am in yours,' replied Dickens brightly.

But as the door of Lady Jane's home closed behind him and he faced the morning gloom, thick flakes of soot eddied around him like black snow, and nothing seemed bright. He made his way from Pall Mall in a hansom cab, through mud and shit so thick and deep that dogs and horses seemed formed from it. People dissolved in and out of the dirty fog like fen monsters, like wraiths, filthy rags wrapped around their faces to ward off the cholera miasma that had carried away six hundred souls only a month before. London seemed all stench and blackness: blackness in the air and blackness in his eyes, blackness in his very soul begging to be white once more as he made his way home to his family.

Family, of course, was everything by that morning in 1854—families alike and unlike, families happy and unhappy—for across classes and suburbs and counties, family had arrived like the steam train, unexpectedly but undeniably. Everybody had to be family and all had to celebrate family, whether it was the young queen and her consort or the poorest factory worker. Like any boom, there were opportunities to be had in family, and just as there were railway speculators, there were family speculators. Few had gambled so boldly and profited so handsomely as Lady Jane, the exemplary devoted wife, or Dickens, the very bard of family. But celebrating family was one thing. Practising it, Dickens had discovered, was something else again.

Because it had been raining too much and he had been gloomy too often, because he felt something too close to failure stalking him like a shadow, because he wanted light and needed to know he was still moving forward in all things, because he felt cold and the cold was growing, that evening he proposed to his wife, Catherine, that they go to Italy the following month. But she did not want to: the children had commitments of one type or another, and besides, her condition, after ten children, did not make travelling a welcome prospect.

Then, after what he felt was an innocent comment from him about her weight, which, as he said, was a simple truth, Catherine abruptly stood and walked out. According to their daughter, Katy, who rushed in soon after, angry at him, at her, at the whole miserable, wretched house they were doomed together to inhabit, along with all the other children, domestics and dogs and birds, her mother had now taken to her bed.

Her bed! thought Dickens, turning away from Katy. Again and again, over and over, back to her bed she would go after every argument, where she would once more become a heaving mound of feather quilt, rheumy eyes and stifled sobs. The last time, he had remonstrated, argued, apologised and, when daring, touched her on her forehead, her cheeks, her lips—but she had recoiled as if bitten by a mad dog. This time he did nothing. Weighing his options, he realised he had none, that somehow something was so broken that no word or action would fix it.

The situation, he knew, was felt painfully by all in the house, a house that seemed to breed only quarrels— between son and daughter, between elder and younger, between governess and servants—the whole house was wracked by a wretched spirit and even the furniture seemed to bear grudges against the walls. There seemed no end to the misery, and, impossibly, everything just went on and on. But that night, rather than fight with his wife, he was mortified to realise that he lacked even the passion to continue the argument.

Rather than go and see her, he put on his coat. A long time ago he had fled from himself into Catherine, but now he was fleeing from Catherine into himself. Then, he had needed her and tunnelled into her to protect himself from all that roamed inside his head, all that he now kept at bay with his ceaseless external activity. It was said he had chosen to marry above himself; but no cynic is ever truly cynical, and he had loved her. But her very presence now brought on in him a wordless anguish. Now he would rather walk to Lands End and back than stay the night in bed with his wife.

He could not bear her misery, nor her listlessness. He could not forgive the way she withdrew from her sacred duties as a wife and a mother into a lethargy that seemed to worsen with each new birth—surely a cause for jubilation, not melancholy?—and how she grew fatter and duller with each passing day. Why did she resort to the grapeshot of domestic life—the caustic aside, the peremptory embrace, the sudden, terrible glance of knowing contempt—and why did he respond with pettiness, with rage, with absence? The worse it got, the less he understood and the more she retreated, and the more she gave ground the greater grew his conviction it was all her fault. Could there be two souls less suited to living together?

His thoughts reformed as the *Erebus* and the *Terror*, thrown up on their sides by the ice, their masts casting diagonal lines across the frozen deep, the wind raising a dirge in their icicle-hatched rigging. And the ice and the cold and keening wind were all him and he was at the same time buried within it; for twenty years, had not his marriage been a Northwest Passage, mythical, unknowable, undiscoverable, an iced-up channel to love, always before him and yet through which no passageway was possible?

And so he decided to go out and, as he so often did now, walk the night away. Walking was his pressure valve, and he the steam engine fit to explode without it. Looking, thinking, improvising scenes, rehearsing monologues and dialogues and inventing plots, he walked miles and miles, ever deeper into the mysterious labyrinth of the greatest city in the world. As clatter, hovels, cries and stench filled his being, he would keep on walking, the filthy dross of the everyday stirring in his alchemist's head and transforming into the pure gold of his fancy.

Once, he had loved to watch and mimic and recall, joining it all in one merge as glorious and muddy as the streets through which he wandered, knowing nothing was coincidence and everything happened for a reason. But now there was a dreariness about all things for him.

There were the 'little periwinkles'—as Wilkie Collins called ladies of the night—to be opened when he went on a jaunt with his friend around the theatres and streets, and though this and all he had ought to have been enough,

35

somehow, for some reason for which he could not find words, it no longer was. Much as he tried to suppress the dangerous, undisciplined thought, he wanted something more—but what he wanted, he could not say.

He felt a curtain lowering on some other world he had visited for a few brief years in his youth: a carnival world, with the brightest of swirling rings, a circus tent he was permitted to enter for a short time only, and for a shorter time yet to be the ringmaster, before being cast out once more into the bootblack night. He was panicked, fearful at the fading of some light he could not describe but which had once illuminated his world.

At some point, he knew, he would return to home and a snoring Catherine. He would fall into a strange slumber in rhythm with his walking: half-awake, half-asleep, possessed of the strangest dreaming. Was it the laudanum he took more frequently of a night to ease his sleep? Or was it just what life had become? Slowly he would feel better, as his characters talked to him, as he came to understand what it was, other than air, that they all wished to breathe.

After a few short hours' sleep, he would awaken before dawn to the sound of carts heading to market laden with produce, and the noise of the streets below his bedroom would soothe him. By some miracle life had not stopped. As he slowly came to his senses, he would again feel an immense surge of relief that, even in the brief hours that he slept, the wondrous world had continued spinning, and he with it.

'It's not her fault,' he heard Katy say behind him, as he went to open the front door.

Startled from his reverie, he turned and looked at her. She was fifteen, a dark beauty and, like him, forceful and quick. He loved all his children, but only with Katy did he share an understanding. She spoke to him in a way no one else dared.

'That Dora died. She was a baby. Maman did all she could.'

'Of course,' he said, as gently as he was able. 'Of course it's not your mother's fault.'

'Sir, the immortal flame of genius burns in his bosom,' Wilkie Collins was saying to John Forster at the Garrick when Dickens, unseen by both men, arrived. They were discussing a scandal involving a well-known painter and two women.

Wilkie Collins had a very large head that teetered on a particularly small body, and the oddity of his looks was accentuated by a bulging left temple and a depressed right temple, so that viewed from one side he seemed a rather different man than when viewed from the other. Outside of an anatomist's bottle, he was one of the queerest things Forster had ever seen. Forster did not like the way Dickens had in recent times taken rather a shine to this odd young man who was, Forster felt, usurping his own position as Dickens' intimate.

'The genius,' continued Wilkie, 'of English—'

'Never mind,' said Forster, 'about his *genius*, Mr Collins.' He said the word as though it were a protracted illness. 'We don't have *genius* in this country unless it is accompanied by respectability. And then, not to put too fine a point upon it, in a word, so to speak, we are very glad to have it—very glad indeed.'

'My dear Mammoth,' said Dickens, coming up behind the two men, placing one hand on Forster's great shoulder before sitting down on the green Moroccan divan next to Wilkie. 'How splendid to see both my fine friends together. Shall we share a sherry negus?'

But Forster was having neither sherry negus nor any of it, and, making some excuses, stood up and left. Dickens seemed unperturbed by his friend's abrupt departure; it was, as he put it after, 'part of the Mammoth's glacial patrimony'. He went on to tell Wilkie about his meeting with Lady Jane Franklin.

'I am rather strong on voyages and cannibalism,' he said, finishing his story.

'And ice?' asked Wilkie.

'Very strong on the ice,' said Dickens, raising a hand to signal a waiter. 'Blue as gin. Sometimes feel I'm shipwrecked there myself.'

Wilkie Collins' nerves were still good; he was yet to invent the detective novel, to be celebrated by his age as one of the great novelists and thereafter forgotten, to have his health fail, to take so much opium to ward off the pain that he would come to believe he had a *doppelgänger*, the Ghost Wilkie. The world for Wilkie was a promise yet to fracture into phantoms, his eyes were yet to turn into bags of blood, and the great Dickens was a friend and mentor. He holidayed with Dickens, he played with Dickens, and he even worked for Dickens on the novelist's magazine, *Household Words*. Life had yet to shape him and he continued to believe he shaped his own life. He was young, quick-witted and, moreover, agreeable to whatever was Dickens' fancy, and when that fancy was periwinkling, Wilkie knew some of the finest halls and houses to frequent. But in this case he was at a loss to know how to agree or what to agree with.

'All those fricassees of the famous beneath mountains of ice, great men meeting noble deaths—do you think it's *exactly* your sort of story?'

'And the kettles,' said Dickens. 'Don't forget the kettles.'

'But only a week ago you said you were about to embark on a new novel and weren't to be burdened with any writing jobs that came between you and it.'

'Well,' said Dickens, 'I've never claimed to be consistent. Besides, I'm weary, my dear Wilkie. I was three parts mad and one part delirious rushing at *Hard Times*.'

'It brought *Household Words* good times,' said Wilkie.

'It left me all done in.'

Wilkie knew that Dickens' magazine, in which his novels would first appear as serials, was more than a major source of income for the novelist. It also mattered that it, as with everything Dickens touched, was not just a success, but an ever greater success.

'I am beyond a novel just now,' Dickens was saying,

'but I need some tale to help sell our Christmas edition of the magazine.' And then, on seeing a bowed, beetle-like figure in a far corner, he brightened. 'Why, it's Douglas Jerrold—he'll give us something.'

On being waved over, Jerrold, his bright eyes bluer than ever beneath huge eyebrows that sat over his sharp little face like watchful moths, was delighted to see Dickens but declined a drink, saying he had been somewhat off-colour the last few months. Instead, he told a short and funny story about sherry negus and Jane Austen's brother, with whom he had served in the navy.

'I read one of Austen's once, I think,' Dickens ruminated. 'Who these days would read more?'

'Macaulay,' said Jerrold.

'Precisely,' said Dickens. 'Unlike you, Douglas, she didn't understand that what pulses hard and fast through us must be there in every sentence. That is why, since her death, she has suffered ever greater obscurity rather than growing popularity—and that is why I really must have you write something for our Christmas edition.'

'If I could, Charlie, I would. But I'm busy with a new play and I couldn't see my way clear to do anything for you till next spring.'

After Jerrold left, Dickens played with his large wedding ring, sliding it off, rolling it around his fingernail. Though he did not say it, something in his meeting with Lady Jane Franklin had resonated in an unexpected and as yet intangible way with him. He could not let it go. He slid the ring back on.

'What do you think, Wilkie, if I did a little paper on Dr Rae's report, taking the argument against its probabilities?'

At his home, Tavistock House, Dickens more closely studied *The Illustrated London News*. Outside, the London morning was almost as dark as night; inside, the hiss of his gas lights comforted him as he read Dr Rae's account. So too, he concluded with relief, did the content. The man had no gift for story.

Dickens put the paper down, moved the bronze statuette of duelling frogs to the centre of his desk and set to work. He opened with some quick, telling jabs, and diverted for a moment to praise Dr Rae deftly, thereby eliminating the possibility of his article being construed as a personal attack.

Then, and only then, in the manner of the barristers he had reported on in his youth, Dickens began to sow doubt over every detail of Dr Rae's account—from the utter impossibility of accurate translation from the Esquimau's argot, to the very real possibility of multiple and even opposing interpretations arising from the savages' vague gestures. He questioned the process of butchering and cooking up a fellow human. '*Would the little flame of the spirit-lamp the travellers may have had with them have sufficed for such a purpose?*' he wrote.

Feeling better with the piece, with himself, with life, he halted, reread this last sentence, and then underlined the phrase *may have had*. The case was building, and he was now feeling words rushing his goose-quill along, leaving trails of ink, blue as ice, leading him and his readers to that strange and terrible world.

He turned to the inescapable matter of the mutilation of the bodies. '*Had there been no bears thereabout, to mutilate the bodies; no wolves, no foxes?*' He didn't answer his own rhetorical question—let the reader answer, he told himself, scurrying straight on to another telling blow.

Would not the men, he now asked, if starving, have fallen prey to scurvy? And does not scurvy finally annihilate the desire to eat and, in any case, annihilate the power? Having readied and teased the reader with his trail of false leads and tempting possibilities, Dickens sprang his trap and revealed what he believed was almost certainly the truth behind the mystery.

'*Lastly, no man can, with any show of reason, undertake to affirm that this sad remnant of Franklin's gallant band were not set upon and slain by the Esquimaux themselves.*'

He paused, his attention momentarily distracted by an odd thought.

'*We believe every savage to be in her heart covetous, treacherous, and cruel.*'

Realising his error, he crossed out *her* and wrote above it *his*. But did these words not sum up his own folly so many years before? And that odd thought took on the form and name of a woman, and Dickens muttered two words.

'Maria Beadnell.'

And how that name irritated him, angered him, enraged

him, reminded him of his wretched origins and the myriad humiliations he had determined never again to suffer. Before he had become Charles Dickens the brilliant, the beneficent and the virtuous genius of letters, he had been Charles Dickens the impetuous, the overly earnest and the not infrequently foolish unmarried youth.

Maria Beadnell. Then, he had presented himself to her banker father as an inferior. He never made that mistake again. His answer to hierarchy was his own uniqueness. He had even refused invitations from the Queen herself. He entered society now at his pleasure, on his terms.

Maria Beadnell, his first love, the mistaken impulse of his once undisciplined heart. And these words, *undisciplined heart*, constantly came back to him—a warning, a fear, the terror of who he might really be. He saw them in dreams inscribed upon the walls of unknown houses, found them appearing unbidden in his writing.

Maria Beadnell and her vile family had treated him as little better than a corpse to play with, to feast upon for their own amusement. Yet looking back, he reasoned that it was his rightful punishment for having given in to his passions rather than keeping them firmly under control. After all, wasn't that control precisely what marked the English out as different from savages?

'*Answer me, undisciplined heart!*' he went so far as asking in one novel. But it never did. And so instead he bound and chained it, buried it deep, and only such severe disciplining of his heart allowed him his success, prevented him from falling into the abyss like his debtor father, like his wastrel brothers; from becoming, finally, the savage he feared himself to be.

Determined to banish these loathsome thoughts from his mind, Dickens attempted to return to Dr Rae and the cannibals, but it was impossible. For now he only had one thought, and that thought one name. And after twenty-five years, Maria Beadnell—now Mrs Winter, married, Dickens presumed, to some acceptable dreariness—had written to him, and they had met at a dinner conveniently and respectably staged at a friend's home.

Love—what of it?

He looked at her withered flesh, her thin lined lips, her bull neck dissolving into the lines of her bosom, crazed as old varnish. She had grown broad and was constantly short of breath, panting like an aged spaniel. Dickens turned to the other guests and said, with a smile and not without ambiguity:

'Mrs Winter is a friend of childhood.'

Once, he had mistaken Maria Beadnell's dull emptiness for enigmatic mystery. And now she, where once contemptuous of him in youth, was flirtatious in middling years—with her 'Charlie this' and 'Charlie that'—how vile it all was! How repellent human beings could be! Fat and dull and full of phlegm, which she provoked into lava-like rumbling with her attempted coquettish giggle, the result was that he caught her cold and lost whatever affection he once had for her.

A few years before, he had even put her in the story that was so much his own, *David Copperfield*, casting her as the one whom David marries: Dora Spenlow. And as he sat there in his study that dark morning, attempting to rescue Sir John, there arose within Dickens another bitter memory he found unbearable: it was while writing this tale of his idealised life, of his unrequited love finally requited, of reshaping the world to just what he wanted it to be, that his ninth child was born and he had named her Dora.

How strange, how eerie he found it, then, when a few months after killing Dora in *David Copperfield*, his own little Dora would die. He had the horrid sense that the world warped to his fancy, but only to mock him in the cruellest way possible.

Outside his study, Dickens could hear his younger children running up and down the corridor, squealing and crashing into walls. He went and shut the second door he had specifically built for the purpose and returned to his desk. The sounds of his family were now distant and muted, but he had lost his train of thought altogether.

He put down his quill, stood and went to a bookcase and searched for several minutes, all the time wondering why he had ever wanted Maria Beadnell. Now he thanked God for her father's prejudice against the lowly. He had a wife, the women of his books, the periwinkles of his nights. It was enough—it had to be.

Dickens' eyes roamed the shelves until finally he found Sir John Franklin's *Journey to the Polar Sea*. After two passes through the book, he found the pages he vaguely remembered; they were, he could now see, even more admirably suited to his purpose than he could have hoped.

Whatever the truth of the book, it revealed Franklin as an infinitely better writer than poor old Dr Rae. Sir John Franklin, Dickens recognised, was surely as fine a creation of Sir John Franklin's own pen as Oliver Twist was of his.

There were several passages in which Sir John recounted how, when utterly reduced by starvation at the nadir of his celebrated 1819 expedition, with eleven of his twenty men dead, there was a level of decency they never abandoned. Rather than countenance the thought of cannibalism, Sir John had eaten his own boots. Dickens felt cheered. That was an Englishman. Stout heart, stewed boots, decency dressed up as diet.

Feeling the pump was now primed, he began to narrate the story: how, when Franklin's first expedition was starving, the Iroquois hunter Michel conceived 'the horrible idea of subsisting on the bodies of the stragglers', probably even killing one or two expeditioners to this end, and how Sir John Richardson then marvellously shot the devil through the head—'*to the infinite joy*,' Dickens now wrote, '*of all the generations of readers.*'

His pen was once more moving in accordance with his fancy, his spirits rising with its life-giving flow. This is what he did! Who he was! He lived and found and knew himself only in story, and in this act of writing Dickens sensed himself becoming joined to Sir John's doomed journey, and to that strange frozen world that held all their mysteries. He thought of how such great spirits as these would always endure stoically to the end, as would he in his marriage. Sir John would not make the error that the

Iroquois Michel was condemned to because of race, that error of passion Dickens himself had once made because of youth. Had he not yearned to bite into Maria Beadnell's thighs as keenly as the Esquimaux had wanted to feast on old Sir John's gentlemanly drumsticks? But the mark of wisdom and civilisation was the capacity to conquer desire, to deny it and crush it. Otherwise, one was no better than the Iroquois Michel or an Esquimau.

The heart of the matter was obvious. The words of a savage could not be taken as the truth, '*because he is a liar*'. Besides, it was clear that cooked and dissevered bodies among this or that tattoo'd tribe proved only one thing.

'*Such appropriate offerings to their barbarous, wide-mouthed, goggle-eyed gods,*' he wrote, feeling rather persuaded himself now on the matter, '*savages have been often seen and known to make.*'

Dickens was worked up now, coming in for the end, music swelling in his ears. His hatred of his long ago inability to rise above his passions somehow became the same thing as the disappointment he felt women had been to him through his life—his mother, Maria Beadnell, his wife, the periwinkles—and he thought of the womanless Sir John with a momentary envy.

'*The noble conduct and example of such men, and of their own great leader himself, under similar circumstances,*' he now wrote, '*outweighs by the weight of the whole universe the chatter of a gross handful of uncivilised people, with domesticity of blood and blubber.*'

He rounded it off with the dying fall of a requiem service,

a tempered oration on why the dead deserve defending and cherishing—God knew, when his time came, he would. He would burn his letters in a bonfire; it would take most of the day. He would create a real double-world stranger than any of his fictions, more convoluted than any plot. He would bind friends to his secrets. He would demand confidences be kept beyond the grave.

And he would pay the cost, immense and crippling, of his ultimate failure to discipline his own great undisciplined heart. It would be the price of his soul.

5

THE PROTECTOR FELT that the vice-regal inspection of Wybalenna had begun particularly well. The beach was covered with Aborigines to greet the Governor, Sir John Franklin, and his party as they landed, leaping and capering with exuberance and shouting exclamations of wild joy. It may not have been elegant or civilised, but it was not without good effect. Lady Jane Franklin was particularly taken with a small black girl dancing in a children's corroborree staged in welcome on the brilliant white sand. The child wore a long necklace of some beauty around her neck and a large white kangaroo skin over one shoulder. She stood out not because of her simple but striking costume, nor her diminutive size, nor her big dark eyes. Rather it was a certain, indefinable attitude.

Lady Jane was unable to bear children; if pressed, she told her friends it had never been a burden, but was, in an odd way, a relief. This was untrue, but over time, like all evasions, it created its own truth. She came to avoid children, and as she grew older—she was now forty-seven—this had transformed into a general unease. There was in them something that she lacked, and which, in her heart, she found terrifying. As if the more of them, the less of her. As though she were dying in proportion to their living.

For their noise and their laughter reverberated too loudly in the empty halls of her memory. She never forgot a younger Sir John asking why she was so white, and herself unable to say anything of that small red stain, for shame and fear. She closed her book, looked up, and told him she agreed with Wordsworth after all, that the sublime was ever to be found in the solitary.

'Is that not so?' she had demanded, her voice breaking shards.

He agreed. He always agreed. More pregnancies ended abruptly. She made life, yet it left her. No one knew. Her life grew incommunicable. There were no death notices in *The Times*. No commiserations, no conversations, no wearing of black. The grief had nowhere to go but inside her. And then time ran out: her body changed. And so now, watching the little Aboriginal girl on the beach, Lady Jane was shocked to sense some intolerable weight dissolving, to feel an unnameable emotion rising.

The child was slightly out of time with the others, but Lady Jane noticed how it was in a way that drew attention to her and her dance, and it somehow seemed only to enhance her performance. Lady Jane was possessed of an overwhelming urge to touch the little girl.

'Why, look,' said Lady Jane, turning to her aged and corpulent husband, 'you almost wish to hold the little wild beast and pet her.'

It was an unexpected observation for them both. She resolved not to let such feelings frighten her. For Lady Jane, what saved the child from being a child was that she was a savage, and what saved her from being a savage was that she was a child.

Presuming the Governor's wife more interested in artefacts than individuals, the Protector explained how the child's necklace was made out of hundreds of tiny, vivid green seashells, threaded on several yards of possum sinew, then wrapped around her neck a number of times. When he went on to say that the necklace had belonged to the child's mother, who had passed away some years before, and the white kangaroo skin to her father, who had died only the week before, Lady Jane was all the more taken.

'The dear little waif,' she said.

'Leda,' said the Protector. 'Her name is Leda. Seven years of age. Youngest on the island.'

'And what eggs, Mr Robinson,' Lady Jane smiled, 'do you expect her to bring forth for posterity?'

'Eggs?' asked the Protector, slightly confused. 'I meant the child, not a chook.'

'You must protect her from swans,' said Lady Jane, making small mischief.

'I'm sorry, Ma'am,' said the Protector, whose knowledge

of classical mythology extended little beyond the names contained in his battered copy of *Carswell's Classical Names & Almanac*.

'Leda,' said Lady Jane.

'Yes,' smiled the Protector. 'A beauty in the ancient world.'

'The ancients believed that, in order to rape the beautiful Leda, Zeus transformed into a swan.'

'Marvellous tale, of course,' laughed the Protector, utterly appalled by the story, by Lady Jane's frank language and, above all, by the exposure of his own ignorance. 'The divine ancients!' he sighed. 'Such stories! Mind you,' he quickly added, as the children ran past them at the dance's end, 'we prefer to call her Mathinna.'

Lady Jane, who never normally touched children, reached out and took Mathinna by her arm. The child wheeled around grinning, till she saw the white woman who had caught her.

'You dance beautifully,' said Lady Jane.

And suddenly embarrassed by the odd spontaneity of it all, Lady Jane dropped Mathinna's arm. The child ran off and the Protector began talking about the new cemetery they were to inspect. But the mix of spirit and tragedy in one so young intrigued Lady Jane.

Certainly her pity, when aroused, was a profound and terrible emotion. Or perhaps she simply found the idea of watching the children preferable to looking at a cemetery. For whatever reason, she insisted the children return and perform one more dance.

Watching Mathinna again, Lady Jane felt she understood the child. She imagined her grief, her needs, her dreams. Afterwards, Lady Jane set a fierce pace as they walked up the hill to the graveyard, leaving Sir John huffing and puffing some distance behind. The Protector, running back and forth between the two, although relieved to find them as one in support of his work, did notice that Lady Jane's mind seemed elsewhere. She was thinking of Mathinna's dancing, her slow way of moving, so distinct and so poignant.

'One might almost say,' she said to Sir John when he finally caught up to her at the cemetery gate, 'her body thinks.'

Sir John's body, on the other hand, gave no more appearance of an active intelligence than a well-tended pumpkin. Yet Lady Jane had long sensed there was within him some mechanism or spirit, some passion, waiting to be set in motion. In private she had at first called him Bear, because that was how she imagined him: a great bear in hibernation. But over a decade into their marriage, she was still waiting for him to awaken, as she fluttered moth-like around his eminence.

Small as he was large, Lady Jane might perhaps have been beautiful had she chosen to highlight her features. But it was as if she retreated from them. And if that were not exactly the case, it was true that her nature was permanently at odds with itself. Her desire for conformity and approval, which she had inherited from her mother, the daughter of impoverished gentry, was at war in her with the vitality and belief in self that she learnt from her father, a northern midlands mill owner. Like her mother, she had married to better herself, settling on an ageing polar explorer who was, at the time, being lionised by London society as the nation's greatest since Drake and Raleigh; like her father, she came to see that Sir John's dullness, as with coal, was only good if it could be burnt to power something larger.

She talked to him of history, landscapes, picturesque ruins and her sensation of vertigo when, as a child, she gathered with vast crowds of the lowliest of London to watch Byron's funeral parade and thought she might fall forever. He replied with reports of navigation, Admiralty regulations, auroras, and how delightful reindeer tongues were to eat when properly cooked, the skin peeling off like a sock. They had nothing in common other than a respect for ritual. The prospect of eating something redolent of feet notwithstanding, she liked his seriousness, which she mistook for an achievement in which she might share.

But he was boredom from the beginning, and if it was difficult to square the romance that surrounded his name with the torpor of his company, it was clear that he was malleable and that she could become the principal creator of his reputation. She resolved to be both his muse and his maker.

Lady Jane's aspirations came from the same source as her shame and her energy: her father. Intimacy between herself and Sir John she had discouraged from early in their marriage. It disgusted her, his sounds and flesh and face, and reminded her of all that she had devoted her life not simply to forgetting but to burning out of her being with experiences of a higher nature. Occasionally he forgot himself and was captive to his basest urges: at such times she believed herself exemplary in her tolerance of the revolting bestiality that is man. She endured his clumsy dull repetitions, the finger exercises of one tone-deaf to flesh. She came to see men as weaker—depraved, certainly—and in servitude to an uncontrollable animality, which was only the more mocking in her case because it had never resulted in a living child.

And so she believed in him: because she had no other choice, because she was already ageing, and because after her initial disappointment with both his dreariness and his lack of vigour, she found him unexpectedly amenable to being dragged along in the wake of her ambitions and passions. His chief virtue, she came to realise, was endurance. It was this that had enabled him to survive the horrors of the Arctic in his famed expeditions of 1819 and 1821, and it was this that made him go along without demur or comment with all her dreams and plans. He was her dancing bear.

For this reason, he offered no resistance to her various schemes, which included a plan to rid Van Diemen's Land of snakes by paying—out of their own pocket—a shilling for every skin brought in; until, £600 poorer, with snakes still abundant and the previously unknown profession of snake breeder firmly established, the scheme was abandoned. And though he had no interest in it, for the same reason he had agreed to visit the Aboriginal settlement on Flinders Island. Lady Jane had declared the Van Diemonian Aborigines there a scientific curiosity as remarkable as the quagga roaming free in the Ménagerie du Jardin des Plantes. And so the vice-regal party now found itself sitting down to dinner in the Protector's cottage, while listening to the Protector's grand and—it had to be said—rather lengthy tales of his historic mission of conciliation.

'His was the kingdom of the great mountains and wild rivers,' the Protector was saying as the plates of the second course, roast wallaby, were taken away. 'The sylvan forests and sublime beaches of western Van Diemen's Land.'

Believing heft was created in spaces of silence, he had learnt to hold a table by pauses as much as by speech, confusing the politeness of others with growing rapture. He let his gaze sweep up and down the distinguished party seated at his dining table that evening—Sir John, Lady Jane, a half-dozen flunkeys and lackeys—and then his own court: his son, his wife, and the Catechist, Robert McMahon, who, since the tragic drowning of his pregnant wife while disembarking in a wild storm, dressed in the filthiest rags. Did any of them, the Protector wondered, have the slightest idea what work it was to create such a grand tragedy with yourself at its very heart?

'He was a king, you see,' he said finally, raising a hand

to amplify his grand tone, for it was as if he were talking of places and people long since lost to another epoch—the Middle Ages, the Norman invasion, Viking axes glinting dawn sun down a river mouth—worlds only vaguely divinable through a swirling maelstrom of myth and lofty phrases. And though all knew well that he was talking about people and events not even a decade old, it was, the Protector realised, already another era, and he was both its Norseman, its final destroyer, and its Bede, its only chronicler.

'And you intended remaking such fallen emperors here as stout yeoman?' asked Lady Jane. 'Does science, Mr Robinson, allow of such things?'

The Protector had begun what he termed his 'friendly mission' with a vague hope hardly worth calling an ambition. He was possessed by a desire he could scarcely grasp. After it ended, he did not understand what had happened. One world had ended and another begun, and he was no longer moving through that old world in wonder, but trapped at Wybalenna, in a new horror he could not escape. He smiled. He held out his hands.

'God decrees such things, Ma'am. How can science disallow it? Besides,' he continued, 'he were much attached to me. First met him in 1830.'

He said this as though it had been in a newly fashionable London club. But this monarch was not sitting in some darkened corner of the Athenaeum in the heart of the greatest city in the world. Nor was he known as King Romeo, a name he would only be given by the Protector in another time in another world, an absurd, upside down, bastard imitation of England. The story the Protector went on to tell was of courage and nobility, the childlike fear of savages, the tale of a family finally saved. But King Romeo's true story was something entirely different.

Then, his name was Towterer. He was standing atop a boulder scree on an unknown mountainside in the middle of a vast, unmapped wildland. Maps were, of course, unknown to him. And if he had been shown one, he would have thought it ridiculous. For he lived not on an island, but in a cosmos where time and the world were infinite, and all things were revealed by sacred stories. He was a tall, powerfully built man, careful and wary, and over one shoulder he wore a white kangaroo skin. Heading towards him along a distant ridgeline was a party of men whose coming he had feared, but of whom he was determined not to be frightened. The sacred stories foretold no tragedy; and besides, he trusted in his own guile.

Then, the Protector was not yet the Protector. Though a handful hailed him by another moniker as the Conciliator, most whites knew him as George Augustus Robinson, a name the blacks abbreviated in their fashion to Guster. And it was while dreaming of himself as the Conciliator yet answering to the name of Guster that Robinson, in company with his band of tame blacks, now advanced up the ridgeline to parley.

Cold rain blew hard, Robinson's party were lousy

with vermin, and their low spirits were compounded by a loathsome distemper. They had for a month made their way through that astonished earth with the intent of bringing in the remotest tribes, but had captured none. They had forced passageways through cold rainforests, lost themselves in cloudgardens of hanging mosses ribboning the sky, trekked along vast beaches stunned by angry oceans that rose and fell like liquid mountains, climbed ranges aching with desolation at the endlessness all around. But only now, as they greeted the tall black man, did it seem their luck had changed.

Towterer was cautious in his reply, saying little, but he made Robinson and his party welcome. He took them into a gully, along a creek and to a forest clearing, in which was a village, typical of the western tribes, formed of a small collection of thatched cupola huts that could each house up to twenty people. Yet Towterer's band was only thirty strong—or thirty weak, depending on how one viewed it. Perhaps, Robinson had thought, the white man's plagues that were laying waste to the blacks in the settled districts in the east had already arrived, a hideous harbinger of his arrival.

The rain slowed, then ceased altogether, the clouds gave way to a night sky studded with stars, and a large fire began to roar. The natives felt Robinson's limbs all over, trying to ascertain if he had bones, if he were a ghost. They made him blacken his face, as though this somehow made him acceptable. Then all the blacks, wild and tame, began dancing and singing in the forest. Finally Robinson gave in to their cajoling and, though awkward and embarrassed, joined in. An aurora swept across the southern heavens, waves of pure spirit, roiling bands of red and green light that rolled through the universe. Towterer became insistent that Robinson take off his clothes. Overcome by a logic he didn't understand, Robinson stripped.

He was momentarily beset by the terrifying idea that this was what he truly desired in life. Naked, he found himself leaping, stamping, flying, lost in a strange abandon beneath the southern lights. Was this his true reward, rather than the money he would be given if he brought all the natives in?

Later he would recall it as ridiculous, but then, as he leapt and yowled, as the flames flared and he felt their disturbing heat on his naked thighs and groin, he did not know, he could not say. That night the universe had flowed into him, he was open to everything, he was alive to other humans and to himself in a way he had never known. That night he felt suspended between the stars and the mountains, the forests and the fire. The dance was dizzying, a thing both wicked and exhilarating. It made no sense. It was beyond understanding. For a moment—perhaps the only moment in his life—Robinson felt freed into something beyond himself.

It could not last.

When he had gone to his tent and saw Governor Arthur's letter of commission folded at the front of his diary, Robinson was abruptly reminded of what was expected of him and who he really was. The very reason he was there would not allow any resolution of the matter other than his capture of these blacks and the bringing of them into a world in which he was only marginally more welcome than they. And all this was so he might make something of himself and his family, so he might rise and be celebrated as a man of standing and repute, welcome in the drawing rooms of polite society, a world where no one danced naked and no one opened themselves to others, and where all practised closing down themselves and everything around them.

He felt as doomed as his fellow dancers.

And as these thoughts had befuddled his brain, Robinson's head grew heavier. His mind, ordered by religion, could only conceive of such disorder as heresy. He was filled with thoughts he knew were not just blasphemous but Satanic. He wondered if God existed only as the ultimate obstacle between a man and his soul. And then only the memory of the wild red light of the fire playing on all their bodies had remained, along with their strange chanting, and then he was asleep.

Robinson had woken suddenly before dawn, aware of an unpleasant presence. He sat up and instinctively turned to see a young native woman sitting behind him, at the head of his tent, clearly keeping watch on him. When he tried to shoo her away, she pointed with a long stick at the knapsack in which he had hidden his three pistols.

They had known all along.

How he rued carrying the pistols! They did not trust him, he realised, no matter how often he protested his good intentions, his desire not to take captives, no matter how much tea and bread he fed them, no matter that he had even shed all his clothes and joined with them in their licentious nakedness. He had never intended turning the firearms on the natives—he had seen what a disastrous failure that had been. The pistols were purely for self-defence, for use in the final extremity.

His way was otherwise—persuasion, reason—because at the back of his arguments were always the men with guns anyway. Why flourish and fire them when others would do that for you? Robinson's was one of many roving parties out in the bush looking for natives—but was his not the only one that promised life, not death?

When morning came, the women of Towterer's tribe were gone. Towterer said they had gone fishing. But by nightfall they were still not returned. Towterer continued listening carefully to Robinson's arguments as though the disappearance of half his people were of no matter.

Through the interpretation of his native lieutenant, Black Ajax, Robinson told Towterer how, in this war the Aborigines could no longer win, he was offering the last and only realistic option left: sanctuary on the islands of Bass Strait in return for their country. There they would be kept in food and provided with all the good things of the whites' world: clothing, shelter, tea, flour, God. He was so persuasive he almost believed himself. On the second night, the forest again reverberated to their singing and dancing, Robinson again went to bed, and again he awoke abruptly before dawn.

But this time there was no sentry posted at his tent. The wild blacks had all vanished into the night, without even waking Robinson's own natives. Towterer's people would not allow themselves to be taken captive by any amount of lies.

When Robinson returned to the southwest three years later, everything had changed. What blacks hadn't been exterminated in the war, Robinson had caught and sent to a holding camp on Flinders Island that would become Wybalenna. Only a few natives in the remotest wilds still remained. The authorities viewed it as utterly necessary that they all be brought in, so that the threat of a resurgent black resistance be once and for all ended.

Robinson instructed his tame natives that the demonstration of force was now permissible in order to obtain their final goal. Now his small white entourage flourished guns and his blacks hardened their wooden spearheads in the fire. In the midst of a storm that seemed without cease, Black Ajax struck out south with a party of blacks, while Robinson waited, after giving his order of just one word.

'Towterer.'

For Robinson had not forgotten the southwest chieftain, nor his careful, clever evasion. Unlike so many others, he had been neither compliant nor conned, nor so foolish as to either attack or run, but brave enough to engage with friendship, and cunning enough to leave in silence.

A week later, Black Ajax and his men returned out of the greyness of falling sleet with eight wild natives.

Towterer was not amongst them. But hung around Black Ajax's shoulder in the form of a sling was a fresh kangaroo skin. He came up to Robinson and swung the sling around to his chest. Inside its grey blood-sleeked skin was a small child, not even a toddler. It was Towterer's daughter.

Black Ajax told of how his armed party had ambushed Towterer and the greatly reduced remnants of his band in the midst of a storm, and he claimed Towterer had abandoned the child in order that he and his wife, Wongerneep, could escape.

Robinson recorded Black Ajax's improbable story in his diary. But he didn't believe it. He was confident Black Ajax had abducted the child to bait the trap. He admired his cunning and respected his diplomacy in concocting the story of abandonment.

The following day the weather had cleared not long after dawn: dirty clouds scurrying away to leave the sky an intense, if chill, blue. Changed, too, were Towterer's people, who had grown surly and restless. Fearing they would escape, Robinson ordered his men to form lines either side of them, the tame blacks with readied spears and the whites with loaded guns. Under this armed guard, Towterer's miserable people were marched to a standing camp at Hell's Gates.

It pained Robinson to have to intimidate them. His head had ached from the necessity of it; his stomach had swirled at the sight of it.

'*They are to me always*,' he had written in his diary that evening, '*objects of the greatest commiseration*.'

He felt the need to pray, but as he put down his quill, he felt a warm, squeamish sensation in the seat of his trousers and realised he had shat himself. He felt weak, but his mind was clear and calm. He determined to eat nothing until his stomach was once more firm; then he would head south to capture the last natives himself. He knew it would not be difficult. After all, he had their child.

At dawn two days later he set off with his son and four tame blacks, following the ground burnt by the Aborigines to construct their passageways through the forests and moors. They had only walked a day and a half when Towterer and Wongerneep were spied on a tableland. After ordering the rest of his party to lie down, Robinson approached them with just a black woman to act as a translator.

Towterer's manner with Robinson was much changed from their first meeting. He seemed overjoyed to see the white man, and he told Robinson he regarded him as an old and dear friend. Finally Towterer asked about his daughter. Her name, he said, was Mathinna.

'She is already learning prayer,' Robinson told him. 'Her future is bright indeed.'

Towterer said he esteemed Robinson in every respect equal to his own family. Towterer was inventing a new idea of equals with which to endure and, perhaps, to battle his subjugation. If it were an illusion, it was also an attempt to deny the terrible cost of reuniting with his stolen daughter.

'I view you and yours no less,' said Robinson. 'So much so, I wish you to come with me and join with your daughter, and together we can embark on the miracle of a new life.'

If there had been something forced about Towterer's effusive behaviour, Robinson could see that there was also something entirely genuine: an understanding that this was a new way in which they would henceforth behave towards one another. For Towterer wanted his daughter, and he was no fool, and Robinson wanted Towterer, and Robinson was Towterer's only path back to his child. Robinson felt his stomach settling.

On a blustery morning four days later, the brig *Gulliver*—chartered to transport such natives as Robinson had captured to the growing Aboriginal settlement on distant Flinders Island—finally came into view, sails full with the warm northwesterly.

'*They are to me always,*' he began writing in his diary that night, glancing out of his tent at the pitiful remnants of a race waiting to be exiled from their native land. But he halted and crossed out this beginning. '*Capt Bateman arr. 5pm. Wind nnw,*' he began again.

Bateman told him that thirteen blacks had died in as many days at the Flinders Island settlement. Robinson entered this in his diary, but not Bateman's final comment.

'They're dying like flies.'

Bateman declared himself astonished with Robinson's ongoing success. Robinson found his stomach, his head, his mood, improving markedly. He forgot about dancing under the southern lights.

'*With me,*' Robinson wrote, '*veni, vidi, vici applies.*'

Wongerneep's death, a year after they arrived at Wybalenna, rather than depressing her daughter, had the oddly opposite effect: the toddler became more friendly, more lively, more curious of what others were doing. And this in spite of the Protector's fury when he discovered that, instead of a Christian burial in his cemetery, Towterer had taken Wongerneep's body to the top of Flagstaff Hill and there built a fire on which he cremated his wife. Mathinna had watched the smoke rise towards the stars and make the moon tremble as, below, her mother charred and turned to ash.

Thereafter, Mathinna seemed always to be around the feet of adults, as if seeking a new mother, but even at such a young age she had the wit to be helpful rather than troublesome. And so she grew into a lively child who seemed unaffected by the growing gloom and listlessness that infected the settlement of Wybalenna, listening to her father's stories of a cosmos where time and the world were infinite, and all things were revealed by sacred stories.

'And this nigger, Mr Robinson,' asked Sir John, 'Tuttereramajig or whatever—you say he had majesty about his bearing?'

In answer, the Protector, his bowdlerised account of meeting Towterer complete, and having revealed almost nothing of what actually took place, stood up, went to a sideboard and picked up a straw-coloured wooden box that looked as if it had been made for a hat.

As though it were some sacred sacrament, he brought

the box up into the candelabra light that radiated across the table.

'It is the Van Diemonian timber, Huon pine,' he said. 'Made under my supervision by Marc Antony.'

There was a scraping of table legs on the wooden floor as the diners, like the tentacles of a startled sea anemone, pulled abruptly inwards to better see such a wonder.

'He looked like a Saracen,' said the Protector, 'and carried himself like Saladin.'

He opened the box's lid. The table stared wordless as an irreconcilable form shaped in and out of the greasy shadows, until finally it took on the undeniable reality of a human skull.

'I give you King Romeo, last of the Port Davey kings.'

After several moments of low murmuring, Lady Jane, delighted with her gift, and even more so with the story of its provenance, which established their skull—as she now thought of it—as one of the finest specimens of its race, thanked the Protector for 'such an especial gift' and grew animated.

'And this King Romeo,' she said, 'he was the father of that pretty little girl we saw dancing earlier this afternoon?'

'He was,' said the Protector.

'And that dear little girl then has neither mother nor father, nor family?'

'She has family, Ma'am, but none immediate. They think of such things more loosely and more intricately than we. For us family is a string, for them it is lace.'

'She is an orphan, though.'

'By our reckoning,' said the Protector, 'she is an orphan.'

'No one can doubt your good work here, Mr Robinson,' said Lady Jane more loudly, as outside one dog began barking, then another and another, until the whole settlement's seemingly infinite population of half-starved curs was yelping. 'But what firmer proof of the worth of your approach could be demonstrated than to raise just one individual with every advantage of class and rank?' She turned to her husband. 'Don't you think so, Sir John?' she yelled.

Sir John mumbled a startled assent, the dogs ceased yowling, and, settling into a steadier, more assured rhythm of speech, Sir John declared that it would be an experiment of the soul worth making, both for science and for God.

'If we shine the Divine light on lost souls, then they can be no less than we,' he said. 'But first they must be taken out of the darkness and its barbarous influence.'

Before arriving, Lady Jane had requested in writing a scientific specimen—a skull from what she termed 'the vanishing race'—and this the Protector had been happy to accommodate. But as he had decapitated, flensed, boiled up and rendered down his friend's skull, glad to know that it was going to such fine people of keen scientific mind, he had not anticipated the request now made across the dinner table. As a further course of roast black cygnets was served, Lady Jane announced she wished to adopt a native child, as though it were the final item to be ordered off a long menu.

'She will be as our own daughter,' said Lady Jane.

'I will choose—' began the Protector.

'You misunderstand us,' said Lady Jane, smiling sweetly. 'We have already chosen.'

And it was then that Lady Jane named the child she wanted above all others, the one she had watched dancing in the white kangaroo skin.

'Her,' she said. 'Mathinna.'

6

BUT WHAT OF DICKENS? For those who had followed the greatest mystery of the age, the prospect of the most popular writer of the day putting forth his view on the sensation of the rumours of cannibalism was irresistible. 'The Lost Arctic Voyagers' was published in *Household Words* just in time for Christmas 1854—no better time, Dickens told Wilkie one evening, to be comfortably warm, kindly thinking of those who were wretchedly cold. Dr Rae's poor prose proved no opponent, the piece triumphed, the edition sold exceptionally well, and Dickens' argument won the day: if Sir John had perished, it would have been nobly, gloriously, heroically; not as a goggle-eyed barbarian.

Thus did Dickens ally his name with the salving of an empire's anguish, and no one was ungrateful. On this basis, Lady Jane donned black mourning. Her life's work of turning her dull husband into a great man, finally relieved of his ongoing and colossal ineptitude, began to bear fruit. Dickens spoke at fundraising dinners she organised for yet more rescue expeditions, the goal—with the favourable absence of evidence—now to proclaim Sir John's undoubted success in finding the elusive Northwest Passage.

Less successful were Wilkie Collins' attempts to raise his companion's spirits through drinking and periwinkling. A taint was upon Dickens. For, having dispensed with Dr Rae and the cannibals, he could not himself escape the growing sense that some greater authority seemed to have turned the whole world into a gaol yard. No matter what accolade or geegaw of success or standing came his way, whatever compliment, congratulation, ovation or award was granted him, all iron was rusty and all stone slimy, all air stank and all light was fading. Still, there was for him only one way, and that way was forward, ever forward, never stopping.

By autumn he had begun a new novel raging against government men and government absurdity, the heart-killing world of government regulations and government offices, and at the end of it he was even angrier and sadder and more lost in the thickening ice floes of his own life. For once, words had not rescued him, great as the success of *Little Dorrit*—as he had called his new novel—was proving in serial.

He continued with his marriage. He continued to believe that, like everything else in his life, it would be righted by the sheer force of his will. He had trouble staying in the same room as his wife, but he stayed nevertheless. He continued to argue in his writing for domesticity, and tried not to think that perhaps this was the very thing in life that had escaped him, that perhaps it did not really exist, or, if it did, it was just one more prison bar.

He kept seeing the cold whiteness of the Northwest Passage, and he kept feeling himself trapped in it with Sir John's corpse. He kept dreaming he was one of a party of lost sailors, making their wretched way through a polar world both terrible and extraordinary, who finally stumble on Sir John's iced ship. Here, they know, is salvation, for here there will be warmth and food; here there will be those who know how to find their way home. But a search of the silent, chill cabins reveals only frozen corpse after frozen corpse.

Something was guttering within him, no matter how he fed the flame. He chose to embody merriment in company; he preferred solitude. He spoke here, he spoke there, he spoke everywhere; he felt less and less connection with any of it. He walked more than ever, he travelled overseas ever more; yet on the inside he felt as still as a seized cog. Nothing moved.

He resolved to live a year in solitude in the Swiss Alps with monks and St Bernards. He resolved to move to Australia. He resolved to escape from himself, yet there was no escape. He felt such pity for the beggars and the downfallen he saw everywhere, the ragged people to whom he often spoke, but he could not understand why his wife, to whom he now almost never spoke, seemed fearful and sullen, why she spoke little to him, and why, when she did, it was so often sharp. He suspected he hated himself. He felt he might burst if he did not press on.

On the train to Dover, he read a whaling captain's description of how, at a certain point in winter in the polar regions, the drifting pack ice joins together into one frozen mass, and any ship so unfortunate to be trapped is unable to move and is squeezed tighter, ever tighter, and everyone waits as the turpentine drips out of the boards slowly being crushed, everyone listens to the ache of the tormented timbers, everyone can do nothing but wait, not knowing if the boat will break and they will then die. It could have been a description of his own life.

'I believe no two people were ever created with less in common!' he cried out to Wilkie on the Montmartre one evening, as with a noisy crowd they watched two Turks wrestling: one large and covered in filthy scabs, the other small and oddly tenacious. 'It is impossible . . .' For a moment he seemed lost for words. 'There is no interest, empathy, confidence, sentiment, tender union of any kind,' he said dully, as if he were reporting on the effluvium of a cesspit.

Wilkie did not know what to do—to express sympathy would be to encourage what perhaps should not be encouraged, rash words that might later be regretted; not to react was to look callously indifferent to what was clearly consuming the man. Fortunately, before he had decided how he would respond, Dickens was again talking.

'It is an immense misfortune to her,' he said, shaking his head, seeming to be uncharacteristically bewildered. 'It is an immense misfortune to me. She is the only person I have ever known with whom I cannot get on somehow or other. I know I have many . . . faults . . .' He shook his head again, as if he were working on a jigsaw puzzle in which pieces cannot be made to fit. '*Which*,' he said, and now tried to soldier on, 'belong to my exercise of fancy. But I am patient and considerate at heart, and I would have beaten out a better journey's end than we have come to, if I could . . .'

Again Wilkie was faced with the impossibility of knowing how to respond, and for a second time Dickens recovered and went on, but in a darker, more bitter, more determined strain, saying Catherine had never overly cared for her children and showed little affection. In front of them, the scabby Turk finally pinned his opponent to the ground. Around them, the crowd roared its approval, then laughed when the Turk spat on the face of his compatriot.

After the evening of the Turkish wrestlers, Wilkie did not hear Dickens speak of his marriage again—or not at least until things had reached such a sorry pass that he could speak of little else. In the meantime, Dickens' activity grew even more frantic: he walked more and more, slept less and less; he attended ever more events and took on ever more burdens. He found himself, one evening, sitting with Wilkie in a Covent Garden theatre watching *Romeo and*

Juliet. The mingled reality and mystery of the show, the poetry, the lights, the company, the dazzling changes of glittering and brilliant scenery, so delighted Dickens that when he came out onto the rainy street at midnight, he felt as if he were tumbling from the clouds into a rancorous world of mud and noise and misery.

To delay that fall a few moments more, he tried to lift himself back up by talking of his next amateur theatrical, which he staged every new year at Tavistock House. Family and servants and friends stood in for actors. Money from the tickets was given to one worthy cause or another, and Dickens' productions had become quite an event in the London calendar.

'The problem is that the year is creeping by,' said Dickens to Wilkie, 'and I still have no idea what our next play might be.'

As the two headed down a dingy street toward a house recommended by Wilkie as 'particularly excelling in sybarite pleasure', the confusion of splendid deaths at the end of the play they had just watched and Dickens' keen interest in Franklin's expedition came together in Wilkie's mind to suggest a solution.

'Wild ideas are on me again, Wilkie,' Dickens was telling his companion. 'Wilder than ever, of going to Paris— Rouen, Switzerland, anywhere—somewhere I can write aloft in some queer inn room. I'm restless, Wilkie.'

'Imagine,' began his companion, 'if your next Twelfth Night play had as its setting that chill, white world.'

'I need a change, Wilkie, but I am obliged to live in a

home with a wife. They say Christ was a good man, but did he ever live with a woman?'

Wilkie coughed.

Wilkie liked women. He found Dickens' railing against women difficult. Unlike his older friend, he was neither sentimental nor conventional about them, and he would come to manage living with two women, without marrying either. Wilkie also had unusual opinions on mesmerism, the spontaneous combustion of human beings, and scrofula, and his opinions on all such matters interested Dickens.

'That world,' continued Wilkie, flurrying his fingers as, in the flaring gaslight, he for a moment beheld not a great man of letters in his prime, but a poor creature preternaturally old, 'where Parry conquered . . .' Briefly he was unsure if the idea had chimed, then he began to suspect it may have been a very bad one. He battled on. 'And where Franklin died.'

Dickens turned and stared intensely at Wilkie, and all Wilkie could hear was the odd sound of him sucking his tongue. Then, in a conspiratorial way, Dickens leant in close.

'Once we're inside,' he said, 'let's order two fingers of their very worst blue gin and five toes of their very best midshipman.'

And Dickens' smile lit up his face, and he turned towards the door as it opened.

'Of course, it is inspired by Franklin,' Wilkie called after him. 'And . . . though the story is a fancy, it is a fancy drawn from the deepest truth. And how much better if it can show Englishmen meeting their ends nobly rather than as savages, their finest qualities triumphing over their basest.'

'Yes,' Dickens said, his back still turned. 'Most impressed. More than impressed. Charmed. A mighty, original notion for a play.' As Dickens led the way up the worn stone steps and the mist around them turned a ruddy yellow from the gaslight spilling out, he looked back, still smiling. 'And you, dear Wilkie, must be the one to write it.'

On entering the house and its warm, enveloping sounds, its overripe scent of cheap perfume, Wilkie had the sense he had simply been given a task Dickens was happy to be freed of.

'You want that line to remain then?' asked Wilkie, when some months later he came to Tavistock House to inspect the improvements being made in preparation for the performance. There was, thought Wilkie, something changed in Dickens since he had seen him a fortnight before.

'Which line?' said Dickens loudly, as the two men made their way along the corridor, advancing into a babel of noise. He seemed to be holding himself differently, with a new vigour and delight in his very posture.

'Where Wardour cries out,' cried out Wilkie, '"The only hopeless wretchedness in this world is the wretchedness that women cause!"'

'You can't makes sense of his character without it,' Dickens shouted back, as though it were another simple instruction of the type he issued daily at the office of *Household Words*, too apparent to demand explanation. Had not women failed him all his life? His mother. Maria Beadnell. His wife. Was it not obvious?

Wilkie coughed.

'Never give in to your stomach, Wilkie,' said Dickens, 'and your stomach will end up giving in to you!' He pointed a heavily ringed index finger at Wilkie. 'Now there's another line that must go in! You see, Wilkie, that is Franklin's experience and his lesson. We all have appetites and desires. But only the savage agrees to sate them.'

And with that, Dickens swung open the door to reveal the chaos and cacophony of a score of carpenters and painters hard at work in a room that bore no resemblance to what Wilkie remembered as the children's schoolroom. Paint pots adorned every available ledge and table, crates of tools lay scattered hither and thither, and at one end a bay window was being taken out and an altogether larger alcove built to house the stage. A labourer was heating size in a great crucible wedged into the fireplace and the room reeked of it, while gasfitters seemed perplexed as they installed extra pipes and lights.

'Is it the Chatham Dockyard?' asked Wilkie.

'It is our theatre,' said a thrilled Dickens, beaming and spreading his arms out. 'The smallest theatre in London but a real theatre nonetheless!'

And then Wilkie realised that not only the room had undergone a transformation.

'I like your beard, Dickens,' said Wilkie. 'Very fashionable.'

Dickens tweaked his newly sprouted whiskers.

'I grew them for the role. I find myself more and more inhabiting, almost living, the part of Richard Wardour. Why, just yesterday I must have strolled the best part of twenty miles, and the best part of *that* was terrifying the locals of Finchley and Neasden into thinking I was a starving and demented polar explorer soon to perish for want of food or warmth, bearded and fully in part. I have it all committed to memory now, Wilkie, every line of yours up here,' he said, tapping his goatish head. 'Do you know what appeals so much about the Arctic?' he said, and smiled once more. 'There are no women there.' And then he was gone to give the gasfitter advice on the placement of a row of jets.

Wilkie coughed.

At first, Dickens had not wished to invest his name in a project that was not fully his. He simply threw his friend ideas for story, a good line here or there. Yet as *Little Dorrit* grew and grew into a prison bigger than it was ever meant to be, the single ray of light shining into his cell was Wilkie's new play.

But it was only after Wilkie suggested Dickens should take the part of one of the play's main characters, a villain to be called Richard Wardour, that his interest quickened. And it was only when he began to see that a man such as Wardour was not half as dislikeable as Wilkie had presented him that he became deeply involved. For Wardour's character interested Dickens, and the more he thought about him, the more oddly close and familiar he seemed. Dickens began stealing time from the final instalments of his novel for *Household Words* to pen yet one more quick letter or card to Wilkie outlining cuts and making changes to his latest draft of the play, which, at Dickens' suggestion, was to be called *The Frozen Deep*.

'What is so marvellous about your play,' he told Wilkie, returning from his conversation with the gasfitter, 'is the way you've created such a man as Wardour—seemingly the worst, but with an unexpected depth. Somewhere near Neasden, I realised that what I must do with Wardour is thaw his frozen deep. I was thinking how we should alter the ending slightly, for he is not all evil—'

'Far from it,' agreed Wilkie, who really didn't agree at all—he had conceived the part of Wardour as a grotesque, of a type that Dickens had so enjoyed playing, to much laughter, in previous Tavistock House plays. That Dickens now saw Wardour as some serious creation, rather than an opportunity to score cheap applause, astonished Wilkie, but, ever open to the undertow of life, he went along with it.

Dickens led Wilkie to a long, dusty table strewn with large rolls of paper, which Dickens unfurled to show his friend sketches and plans for the scenic backdrops. Wilkie murmured the name at the bottom of one sketch in approval. It was no less than William Telbin, the celebrated landscape painter. There seemed no one Dickens had not roped in to lend a hand.

'Wonderful,' said Wilkie, meaning it. His friend's energy, his capacity to invest such industry in even a folly such as this, an amateur theatrical, he always found overwhelming, amusing and oddly moving. 'Simply wonderful.'

'Here, in the first act,' said Dickens, pointing to a sketch of a harbour with a decaying coaching house to one side, 'on the very eve of the departure of a great Arctic expedition, our heroine, Clara Burnham, pledges her undying love to Frank Aldersley—cue applause for Mr Collins—an officer of one of the two ships setting out on this perilous mission. He little knows that on the other ship is no other than Richard Wardour—a role I will seek to inject with a perfectly electric pathos—the ardent admirer Clara once spurned, who has most solemnly vowed to avenge himself on Aldersley for stealing Clara from him!'

'So,' said Wilkie, knowing how Dickens loved to tell and retell his tales as a way of testing their mettle, 'we begin by presenting Wardour as a villain, but as the play progresses, you think it better if he is revealed as perhaps a more tragic figure?'

'He does strike me,' said Dickens, 'as a man forever seeking and never finding true affection. Is that not the case?'

Now dimly suspecting the appeal of Wardour, Wilkie, rather than answering Dickens' question, replied by reinventing the play. 'I have wondered,' he said, 'how moving for an audience it might be if, at the end, Wardour is transformed—if he chooses to sacrifice himself so that the girl he loves wins the man she loves, although it is in Wardour's power to let that same man die and take the girl for himself.'

Dickens was silent, but his lips were moving, as if engaged on some gargantuan piece of mental arithmetic, adding and subtracting, dividing and recalculating. 'A death is good,' he said at one point, 'very good,' and then he went back to his silent mumblings. 'And do you know why?' he unexpectedly demanded of Wilkie. 'Because even Wardour, finally, is not a savage!' His bearded face was beaming. 'Is that not so?'

Wilkie pondered if it was so for a moment. If it had been clear that villainy was previously the very bedrock of Wardour, it was equally clear it no longer was. And what had been meant to be the lightest of entertainments was taking on some other dimension.

'I always felt,' ventured Wilkie, 'that Wardour was so much more than a simple villain.'

Dickens nodded.

'Driven low by cruel Nature,' suggested Wilkie.

Dickens nodded more vigorously.

'Bowed by Fate, undoubtedly,' continued Wilkie, encouraged. 'But a savage, never . . .'

'A savage, my dear Wilkie, be he Esquimau or an Otaheitian, is someone who succumbs to his passions. An Englishman understands his passions in order to master them and turn them to powerful effect. Was and is that not Franklin? And here we have a man *poisoned* by his passions,' Dickens continued, unfurling another roll of paper across which was scrawled *ACT III*, 'but who, at the end, with both ships trapped in the Arctic ice, and horror all around—' Dickens paused. The unrolled sketch showed a ship's deck. Dickens shook his head. 'No, this won't do. Not now. Not with such a dramatic dénouement. We need towering cliffs of ice. The terror of the sublime. Because Wardour finally chooses something far better than allowing his rival to die: he sacrifices himself in order that Frank Aldersley can have Clara—a rather splendid redemption, I think.'

And with that, he picked up a pencil stub and ran a line through the sketch.

So Dickens continued over the final eight weeks, altering lines here, adding monologues there, changing plot everywhere. As the story drifted like pack ice then froze into a fixed shape, he was also attending to the invention of the world of the play—the sets, the costumes, the casting, the props—to such an extent that when the play's programme was published, Wilkie, whose name still appeared as its author, thought it prudent to have added on the title page 'Under the Management of Charles Dickens'.

For Dickens was stage director, very often stage carpenter, scene arranger, light setter, property man, prompter and bandmaster. He had authentic Arctic costumes made for the explorers, employed and trained 'snowboys', whose job it was to scatter paper snow onto the stage from above, and substituted hammocks for the beds to impart the necessary veracity. On his nocturnal walks, he devoted himself more and more to the frozen deep rather than little Dorrit, falling into the part of Wardour, shouting out his lines as he went, walking himself into new lines, venturing farther and deeper into the treacherous shoals of ice that entrapped his own lost soul.

One final matter irritated him, though. *Why* would Wardour sacrifice himself? Somehow, something was lacking in their invention, which insufficiently explained why a bad man would do such a good thing. Then, while out walking one night, he realised Richard Wardour was not bad at all; rather he was good, a good man who might rescue himself—and with what?—with love! Lack of love had iced Wardour's soul, and love rescues his soul from the ice, such a love that he would lay down his life for another!

'Young and loving and merciful,' he cried out to Clerkenwell, Wardour's voice now filling his throat. 'I keep her face in my mind, though I can keep nothing else. I must wander, wander, wander—restless, sleepless, homeless—till I find her!'

And then Dickens halted, puzzled, lost. Who was this woman? She didn't exist. It was all delusion.

In the new year of 1857, after four weeks of full dress rehearsals, a hundred people crammed into the refurbished schoolroom at Tavistock House—among their number members of parliament, judges, ministers and several journalists—to watch Dickens, his family and friends perform *The Frozen Deep*.

The cast was all the old crew—or nearly all, Douglas Jerrold still being unwell—the children, of course, Wilkie, Freddie Evans, Augustus Egg, John Forster, Catherine's sister Georgina Hogarth, who played a Scottish nurse with second sight, and a Scottish servant getting some laughs as an Esquimau. But Dickens stole the show.

He had gone so far as to invite theatre reviewers, and they, along with the rest of the audience, were stunned by the intensity of Dickens' performance, particularly in the closing scenes when, clad in rags, he transformed from a man about to murder his rival in love, to one who, as music specially composed for his death scene swelled and rose, sacrifices himself for that same love.

'He has won the greatest of all conquests,' said Wilkie as Frank Aldersley, standing over his friend's prostrate form. 'The conquest of himself.'

Strangely, as he uttered these, the play's closing words, in that moment preceding the curtain's fall and the rapturous applause that followed, Wilkie felt a growing irony that he thought best to keep to himself.

He soon came to see that success is deaf to irony. Dickens was lauded in *The Times* and *The Illustrated London News* as having the powers of the best of professional actors, while *The Athenaeum* went even further: his performance, it declared, 'might open a new era for acting'.

Shaking her head, Mrs Ternan closed *The Athenaeum* and put it down on the train seat next to her. *A new era for acting!* Opposite, a young man looked askance, for Mrs Ternan was dressed in black mourning, and was—improbably, impossibly and clearly disrespectfully—laughing. The train lurched around a bend and braked at the same time, its whistle screeching, with the effect of throwing everyone in the third-class carriage back and forth. When the train resumed a more settled ride and the passengers their original seating, she contained herself and apologised.

'My sister,' she said. 'We buried her this morning in Salford.' And then she would have burst into tears, if she were someone other than Mrs Ternan. But tears were what she wept on stage; tears were what she worked so hard to elicit from audiences; tears were art and art's reward. This, though, was life. Mrs Ternan's vicissitudes had trained her to laugh at life rather than be broken by it. 'Never,' she said to herself. Though she was a thoughtful woman, she lived by this unthinking mantra. Never ever give in. Never ever complain. Never ever admit to failure.

She crossed her hands in her lap so that he might not see the darned holes in her gloves, inwardly cursed herself for not having warmer clothing to wear in the unheated carriage, and looked out of the misty window as though she could see something of the iced landscape beyond as the train steamed northwards.

Still, the matter of the review amused her, and if it were not for her determination to remain respectable, she would have laughed again. A gentleman and his untrained children in front of a paper house! It may have been some new form of mesmerism, but it most certainly wasn't theatre. And Mrs Ternan most certainly knew what theatre was; after all, she had been treading the boards—damp, rotten, creaking, splintered—since she was three. And though she believed in the theatre of Shakespeare and Molière, it had not repaid her passion. Here she was, she thought, fifty, alone, with three daughters, renting a very small house on the outskirts of London, with little income and, it would seem, diminishing prospects.

It wasn't the life she had expected when, as a young woman, she'd looked to become another Mrs Siddons; when she had made more money than Fanny Kemble in Boston; when she played opposite Charles Kean; when she was celebrated for her acting in both the Old World and the New, and adored for her looks; when she had married a young Irishman of great ambitions—but he had died insane in Bedlam, and she had aged, and the good roles became fewer and the need to take whatever was offered grew stronger. She had journeyed through the provinces, lived on beer and bread and slimy old meat, trudged back and forth between damp lodgings and distant theatres, laid her dead young son out in a cot and then worked three nights in a row, coming home to his cold body each night, until she had enough to pay for his funeral.

She was determined for something better for her three daughters, but it was hard to know what that might be. There was the one-time Infant Prodigy—as she had been billed—her eldest daughter, Fanny, who had so enchanted audiences with her performances as a child but had not been able to carry that magic into her young adult life; there was Maria, ever able, but without overwhelming beauty or talent, equally destined for neither greatness nor fortune. Then there was her youngest, Ellen, who had also been on stage since she was three, who had danced polkas, played boys in tights, performed with acrobats, sang solos and duets and choruses, but who now, at eighteen, had the looks but not the vivacity on stage that might bring fortune.

Times were not good. Fanny and Maria had boldly attempted to set up a school for young ladies the previous summer, another form of fancy; it began with hope and an empty house and ended with neither. Though her friends in theatre helped in finding parts, Mrs Ternan could no longer rely on the Cordelias and Desdemonas that had once brought her a good living. Maria had a fortnight of bit parts at the Regency but nothing beyond it, while Fanny had found steady, if not starring, work as Oberon in a production of *A Midsummer Night's Dream*.

She picked up *The Athenaeum* again, and took out the letter she had used as a bookmark, the letter that bore the news of Louisa's death. She had been just fifty-three, with four children. Mrs Ternan did not know how much longer she might go on before she might suffer similarly—perhaps dying on stage like poor old John Pritt Harley, who had dropped like a stone a few nights before while playing Bottom, with poor Fanny standing right there next to him. And if she died, thought Mrs Ternan, what then would happen to her girls?

For the time being, she was able to continue to trade on the memory of her beauty and past triumphs, on her friendships and the acumen she had accrued over the course of a life of beds shared with children and bedbugs, of cheating theatre managers, threadbare clothes and the illusion of merriment. If she had often to make clear her respectability and virtue in face of a world that viewed her profession as little better than public prostitution, it was also a life not without its compensations: if you could through talent gain the public's favour, you were able, in some measure, to live independent of men, of whom she had a diminishing opinion. It was a better world than that of governesses and seamstresses. But it was still harsh and terrifying, and all that sustained her was the friendship of other actors.

On the night she had received the news of Louisa's death, leaving her the only surviving member of her family, Mrs Ternan had stifled her weeping with a pillow so her daughters would not hear her heart breaking and would never suspect what she now knew: that every death of those you love is the death also of so many shared memories and understanding, of a now irretrievable part of your own life; that every death is another irrevocable step in your own dying, and it ends not with the ovation of a full house, but the creak and crack and dust of the empty theatre. Mrs Ternan felt an infinite darkness beckoning; she resolved only that she would face it bravely. What could a gentleman and his children playing at theatrics know of any of it?

The young man was now looking at Ellen, who had travelled with Mrs Ternan to the funeral and who was sitting at the other end of the bench seat, engrossed, as always, in another novel. With great care, Mrs Ternan had mended Fanny's old out-of-doors dress for Ellen to wear to the funeral; it did not look shabby, nor was its fawn colour—now faded to a dull grey—lurid, but, she felt, entirely respectable. To make it clear that the young attractive woman was not some fallen girl, but a chaperoned young lady, Mrs Ternan held out *The Athenaeum* to her.

'Read this, my darling, and kindly tell me if you think you can ever trust a glowing review.' She passed the magazine over; she was insistent. 'For my money, I think never,' she smiled, thinking how, until the final curtain swept her forever away, she would keep the show going. 'Never ever.'

With the play that had buoyed him for so many months now over, Dickens lapsed into melancholy. He returned to writing *Little Dorrit*. In an ever-growing frenzy, he did not realise he was writing himself. London seemed damper, darker and dingier than ever, and everything and everybody on the streets and on the page felt entombed and dying. As he lived his crowded life, he wondered how it was possible to feel so alone. His solitude terrified him.

He dosed himself more frequently with laudanum. Those who objected that *Little Dorrit* was his gloomiest novel got no argument from him. It was also his most successful, its sales in serial form exceeding all his previous works. He was so alone. He resolved to endure. He would sacrifice all. He could not bear to talk to his wife. He was forty-five. He and Catherine no longer recognised each other, no longer could apprehend in the other pain, sorrow, regret. He could feel something breaking.

Was it the world? Was it him? He had been drawing on something within to keep writing his books, to play Dickens, and it was some reserve he no longer had. His soul was corroding. Certain blows rained down on him, all the more incomprehensible and unsayable because of his external success. It was a slow loss of life, or vitality, or somesuch, some force that joined him with others, and it was that joining with others that he found harder and harder. It was as if the more of him there were in his books, the less of him in life. He might have spoken about it if he knew anyone who might have understood, but, not understanding it himself, that was impossible. He was falling and falling and he did not know how to stop.

Winter gave way to spring. He finally bought Gad's Hill, the home in Kent he had dreamt of owning since, as a child, he walked past it with his father. He remembered himself as a queer small boy listening intently as his father told him that, if he were very persevering and worked very hard, he might some day come to own it. He had persevered. He had worked hard. He had talent—some said genius. He had Gad's Hill as proof. It should have felt an affirmation. It didn't.

Genius—what was it? Increasingly it felt an agony. Yet

only in his work did Dickens truly feel that he became himself, only as he took on the mask of this and that character did he discover the very truth of who he was. His novels were true in a way life was not. Why, even Katy had accused him that his characters in his novels were more real and dear to him than his children. He denied it, he laughed it off, he resented it. He moved his family to Gad's Hill, but he remained most nights in London, sleeping in a small suite he kept above the *Household Words* office. He feared his work was eating up his soul. Talent, genius—were these just names for his determination to continue excavating himself until only a corpse remained to offer death?

He looked in the large mirror he had hung opposite his desk to observe his own face as it played out the part of this character or that. But all he saw was a face that could have been any man and no man, somebody who in his relentless mimicry of everybody had become nobody. He had met most of the great men of his age and been invariably disappointed. I have no peer, he thought. How he missed Richard Wardour!

The rain pattered down erratically, as if troubled by some guilty secret; the city through which he was once more nightwalking was a hundred heavy shades of pewter. Yet it was the only real home he had, wandering those foul rookeries and casual wards, mazes of misery with their half-naked inhabitants and oilskin doors and broken windows, the wretched courtyard where a wraith-like woman drooled as she sucked opium from a rude pipe contrived from a penny ink bottle. Above, he saw the wild moon and clouds rolling restless as an evil conscience in a tumbled bed. Finally light staggered down into the streets of the Great Oven. He made it back to his rooms an hour after dawn.

He went straight to his desk. He felt his thoughts start stuttering and then words spat and fizzed, and one word led to another and then that in turn led more along. In this way, he knew, wars, revolutions, conspiracies, love affairs and novels were made, but nothing could empty Dickens' head of something beyond words: it was fit to burst with everything that could never be said.

'*The wind is rushing after us, and the clouds are flying after us, and the moon is plunging after us, and the wholly wild night is in pursuit of us,*' he found himself writing in his notebook; '*but so far we are pursued by nothing else.*'

It made no sense. Why was the night in pursuit? And who was *us* and *we*? Who would walk with him?

The strange journey to where Dickens would find *us* and *we* began a week later when he travelled by railway from Gad's Hill up to London. A man with a collapsing Stilton for a head entered Dickens' carriage. He sat down, opened a newspaper, then almost as soon as it was fanned out, folded it back up and turned to the passenger next to him. He spoke as though reporting an advertisement for chamber pots.

'Douglas Jerrold is dead.'

Dickens was stunned. Why, he had seen his good friend only the week before, and though Jerrold had said he had been sick, he had put it down to the inhaling of fresh paint from his study window.

It had been a wretched enough morning already. Katy had bought a bonnet and Catherine had felt it perfectly fine. He liked seeing his daughters look as splendid as she did in the bonnet, but the cost! the cost! His children had no idea about money—they were as spendthrift as his own father had been, and, he feared, perhaps as doomed.

He had shouted at Katy, who had shouted back, and then Catherine shouted, then it seemed that there could be nothing said unless it was by shouting. Then he had stopped and in a whisper begged for them all to stop, to stop such madness as this, to stop falling apart, to come together once more as a family. But it was a speech, words, and no one cared a fig for it, and Catherine was weeping again and Katy was standing at her side, glowering at him.

All he could do was try to steady himself by returning to work, to some new project in which he might once more bury himself alive. But *Little Dorrit* was done, the last instalment at the printer, and he had no project before him other than *Household Words*.

By the time Dickens saw Wilkie at the *Household Words* office, his thinking had made several leaps. Knowing there was no private income in Jerrold's family, Dickens proposed to Wilkie that they stage some benefit performances of *The Frozen Deep* for the widow and her children. After all, its initial run of just four performances had caught the attention of London, and had not he and Wilkie both been met frequently with requests to reprise the play from every section of society, up to and including the Queen herself?

And so it was that on the fourth of July, a command performance of *The Frozen Deep* was given at a new, larger venue—the Royal Gallery of Illustration—for Queen Victoria, Prince Albert and their family; among the other guests were King Leopold I of Belgium, Prince Frederick William of Prussia, and his fiancée, Princess Victoria, and even such luminaries as Hans Christian Andersen. This was followed by three additional performances at the same venue over the next few weeks. Dickens was once more Wardour, and his performance an even greater sensation.

'If that man would go upon the stage,' exclaimed Thackeray in the foyer afterwards, 'he would make £20,000 a year!'

But for all the success *The Frozen Deep* enjoyed, despite the expensive ticket prices, insufficient funds were raised to sustain Mrs Jerrold. Dickens, emboldened by his success, his spirits raised by once more playing Wardour, decided to stage a further series of performances in a much larger venue that would hold an audience big enough to raise the money needed. He settled on the Manchester Free Trade Hall, a magnificent new building which could seat two thousand people.

If the size solved one problem, it created another. Dickens became convinced that his amateur actresses would not be able to project their voices sufficiently loudly and dramatically in such a cavernous theatre. Engaging and charming as his daughters and servants were in a small space, where their dramatic failings somehow created a kind of domestic charm, in a great theatre he feared that they would simply be viewed as mediocre, even ludicrous. He would need to find professional actresses.

The working entrance to the Haymarket Theatre was a furtive door protruding into a side alley, from which the summer morning heat was raising a chutney of odours. With the toe of a boot, Dickens flicked aside the oyster shells splattered with bird droppings that were piled over the entrance steps. A filthy urchin, clad in only a torn waistcoat, rode a pig past, chattering in some gibberish Dickens took to be Gaelic, with two other semi-naked children walking alongside. A starling flew out of a hole above the door, to the shrill sound of hungry fledglings, as Dickens entered the dark and rather grim hall. He made his way towards the distant sound of music and dancing feet, to that place he loved above all others, where hearts can be at once disciplined and undisciplined, that world where, given a mask, lies speak the truth.

After twice getting lost, he came upon the backstage, a confusion of beams, bulkheads, ropes and rollers, and such a mixing of gaslight and daylight, of long shadows and short shadows, that none of the natural laws of the universe seemed any longer to apply. And sitting amidst it all, striped by the shadows, was a young blonde woman silently sobbing.

'Why, goodness gracious, Mr Dickens, when you said soon, I did not realise it meant this very morning in the midst of rehearsals!'

Dickens turned to see a sturdy but not unattractive woman.

'Mrs Ternan, I knew you would be busy, but I have a proposal that I wished you to hear as soon as possible.'

He looked back to the crying young woman, whom he now recognised as one of Mrs Ternan's pretty daughters; he had admired her on stage the evening before.

'I'm afraid Ellen here feels that she is undone in the final scene when she must appear in the ripped dress. She feels it leaves too much of her leg revealed. You see, *Mr* Dickens'—and at the mention of his name, Dickens swung around to face Mrs Ternan—'I have trained my daughters to be respectable *and* actresses, and not to view the two as incompatible. They are not common players.'

'Mr Cornford of the Regent's Playhouse spoke very highly of both the character and ability of your family, Mrs Ternan.'

When he had watched Ellen Ternan, who to Dickens looked a pretty sixteen, perform as Hippomenes in a play called *Atlanta*, he had thought she seemed competent. Her calves were also rather attractive. But he understood from Mr Cornford that one of her sisters was outstanding and her mother was much respected, and that all four female professionals were reliable, respectable and, not least importantly, available on the dates the Manchester Free Trades Hall was booked.

'If you wished, I could speak with the manager about costuming . . .' Dickens' eye strayed back to the girl. Her large eyes a piercing blue. Her stockings very thin. Her legs—

'Oh, I need not worry, Mr Dickens. I will have my way and my daughter will not be cheapened; her name and our name will not be so easily lost.'

From the high gallery windows, with their little strip of sky, there fell a strong beam of light. Dickens felt its unexpected warmth, its nourishing goodness.

'No one will speak to the manager,' said the girl suddenly. 'I simply shall play my role as I see fit'—she lifted her head up high with a flourish as she spoke—'and that shall be that.'

'Ruin ought be, if ruin must come, ruinously worthwhile,' said Dickens, knowing he was now playing and not quite able to restrain himself.

Mrs Ternan feared business was being lost.

'And your proposal, Mr Dickens?'

But the girl appeared not to be listening when he replied. She was watching his hands. They darted about like the wings of a wild bird in a cage.

7

ONLY LATER, when he was dying in the resolute black of an Arctic winter, turpentine oozing from the compressed planks of the *Erebus* in which he lay, did Sir John come to see how difficult governing a part-prison, part-bazaar might be. His openness, his indecision, his lack of guile, his absence of secret agents, his ignorance of the necessity of compromise, his patrician disdain for the dark arts of inclusion and exclusion, of favour and persecution, had in Van Diemen's Land doomed him finally to derision and contempt.

Leading the starving remnants of his expedition, he had the previous month reconnoitred to the south, but, failing to find any recognisable landmark in that terrible white, they had returned to winter in their two ships, to make their one startling discovery: the *Terror* already crushed between floes and sunk, only a snapped mast left on the ice as evidence of what once had been.

On finally taking off his frozen boots in Crozier's cabin in the *Erebus*, three toes had come off with Franklin's stocking. They amputated his leg twice, once below the knee and once above, but the gangrene had him.

Outside, the wind roared and necklaces of ice danced through the air. Inside, death seemed welcome, if only because it might relieve him of his own insufferable stench. He understood little of people generally and had, in society, tended to leave them to his wife, who assured him she did. In this, too, he could now see he was mistaken. She simply lacked his humility.

Though Lady Jane would later show an ability for intrigue first awakened in her by the Van Diemonians, at the time she cultivated everything that was opposed to her nature: meekness, servitude, altruism. She was not a raconteur nor yet one taken with stories, be they in a foolish novel or tripping off the tongue of the woman sitting next to her at dinner. Still she tried, for she was in her own soul, as she was in everything, an inescapable self-improver in whose mind Van Diemen's Land and her own ambitions had become one.

Nowhere, Lady Jane had realised on arriving in that colony not yet forty years old, could be more ripe for reform and enlightenment. Her mind ran with ideas for projects and ventures and organisations. The island was prospering as never before, a flood of convict slave-servants tending its ever-growing flocks of sheep, which produced ever more wool for the booming textile mills of Britain. Its people—those not in chains, at least—were ready for a

Golden Age, and when the history of that age came to be written, Lady Jane was determined that she and Sir John would be at its head.

The island of which her husband was effectively monarch at first seemed to Lady Jane a delightful plaything, which Sir John might remake after the image of countless London parlour conversations. And at the beginning he had restructured the convict system in line with the most enlightened thinking, founded learned and scientific societies, and held soirées where matters intellectual, philosophical and scientific were discussed at extraordinary length. His supporters said he never slept, his critics that he had never awoken.

The young daughters of the free settlers, who had loved Government House for the opportunity to dance the night away to the military band, were at first mystified, then angered, when they arrived to discover the ballroom given over to yet one more solemn discussion on the emerging science of mesmerism or the beneficial applications of magnetism to agriculture.

Through her husband, Lady Jane had set about with great enthusiasm founding hospitals, charities and schools, leading the society away from the simple making of money and towards the reason of an enlightened Old World.

'Do you think you could procure for me a pretty little design for a glyptotech?' she wrote to her sister in London, using the fashionable Greek word for a building to house sculpture. 'The island needs its own Ancients and Mythology. I can think of no better way of beginning than with a few rooms of small size, though good proportions, to hold a number of pictures and a dozen casts of the Elgin and Vatican marbles. Expense is an important object, or I shall never in this money-loving colony get the means of erecting it. Could you arrange to have casts made of the Theseus, Ilyssus, Torso and Horse's Head at the British Museum, also the Apollo Belvedere, Venus de' Medici, and the Dying Gladiator?'

'Lady Bluebottle would do better filling her dance card with admirers than the island with the French ideas of the petticoaterie,' her husband's secretary, Montague, sniffed to his Hobart Town friends when recounting her ambition. But in her presence, of course, he only smiled and praised her initiatives.

'Other women seek flowers,' she once told Montague, in whom she correctly sensed piqued influence, 'but I contend for laurels.'

And for a time, her laurels pleased the upper echelons of the island, for, though in various ways dependent in their prosperity and power on the dreary misery of the many, they had nevertheless acquired the habit of defending themselves by garlanding themselves with culture.

For the leaders of Van Diemen's Land weren't objectionable because they had dull poets, pompous naturalists and bad watercolourists, but because, having them, they couldn't keep quiet about it. They recited grating verse, hung their walls with brutal brushwork, gloated about their learned societies and assured each other their several amateur scientists were daily making extraordinary discoveries.

Above all else, they boasted of the couple who seemed to them to embody all that they saw as most splendid and special about themselves: the reputedly dashing new Governor and his wife. They were interesting people, celebrated people who were abreast of the latest fashions of thought, respected people who knew the right people in England, remarkable people who would make greatness of this colony, marvellous people who were exactly the right motley to throw over the mediocrity that really ran the island.

And so they flattered and feigned to the vice-regal couple, and only the women convicts at the Female Factory gave definite expression to what the unfree felt: as Lady Jane lectured them on morality as the basis of all life, they turned their backs and, as one, flicked up their skirts and waggled their dirty arses. Beyond the immediate halo of power, in the outer rings of society, most convicts and ticket-of-leave men paid them no heed. In their sly grog shops and knock-houses, life went on as it had, with their banned songs and wild grog sweetened with sugar; in the backblocks and the forests, in the kitchens and stables and workshops and pits, luck and fate as ever determined whether they lived or died, were raped or flogged or freed, whether they found enough to eat or starved.

But then a great depression swept Europe, the market for textiles collapsed, the mills faltered, the free settlers could no longer get the prices they once had for their wool, and there was no longer gold flowing in abundance. The colony's prosperity was halted and everyone in the colony understood the cause—His Bulkiness, Sir John, and his interfering wife, Lady Jane.

The Franklins were for a long time oblivious. Sir John began a Van Diemen's Land navy with the construction of six gunboats, and was rather excited at the prospect of ordering new cannon with powder and shot. It gave him the illusion he was a man of action, which he felt might compensate for his failure to be a man of intrigue. On his arrival, he had been astonished by the prosperity of the colony. He was received with feasting, balls and every form of public rejoicing. On entering the northern capital of Launceston, he was escorted by three hundred horsemen and seventy carriages, the streets were thronged with well-wishers, all enthusiastic. The tyrant Arthur, his predecessor, was gone. It was as if he were a liberator. He never understood, then or later, Montague's advice.

'No government,' warned his secretary, 'faces such dangers as a despotism when it seeks to reform itself.'

And so, with the boom over, the island suffered and seethed and began planning its vengeance. The Franklins continued exploring, reporting and holding soirées. For Sir John and Lady Jane were keen observers of everything, save the people around them.

Visitors, old colonists and prospective new free settlers alike sailing into the island's capital, Hobart Town, were all momentarily buoyed by an initial enthusiasm, spirits raised by the journey up a splendid estuary full of picturesque wooded hills and romantic little bays that revealed nothing of the miserable lives of those who lived beneath the occasional wisps of chimney smoke rising from deep within the forests.

And how correspondingly large was their disappointment, how their spirits then sank, when they finally came upon the bedraggled town that not so much rose as staggered drunkenly up the cove to the foothills of the great mountain beyond. It seemed to combine the worlds of the army barrack and the prison yard into a town at best monotonous and at worst monstrous.

For the convicts, who were only then dragged up from the sour shitty holds of what had been slaving ships fitted for the far shorter run between Africa and the Americas, there was neither exhilaration nor disappointment. They had survived six months' sailing from the Old World. It was enough to be alive. They took what measure they could of the strange, obscenely fresh air and the vivid, hard blue light, and determined only that they must go on.

It was a walk of but five minutes from the New Wharf to the somewhat ramshackle vice-regal mansion that sat on a bluff to the immediate south. What had begun as a cottage had been extended, then covered over, then added to and covered over again. Much as the colony had grown from a few hundred souls desperate for survival to a society of forty thousand, skin upon skin the cottage grew, until a great onion of a building had arisen. The island's capacity to transform everything into unreliable memory even before it happened, or in spite of it never happening, was already apparent in that crumbling edifice, which, though only thirty years old, was already a relic of magnificent decay.

But when Mathinna finally arrived there the spring following the Franklins' visit to Wybalenna, after a journey that had taken far too long, her eyes did not see the rising damp, the peeling paper, the cracked and patched plaster, the pitching building that left door and window frames rising and falling like so many winking eyes. She saw instead a palace of the type she had heard the Protector describe. Even its musty smells of dead huntsman spiders and stale possum piss she understood as being what the Protector had told her so much about: the fragrance of God.

Mathinna Flinders—as she was entered in the ship's log, for the captain, being only semi-literate, believed writing was above all an exercise in decoration and felt all his passengers needed a second name to balance their first—had taken ten days to sail from Flinders Island to Hobart Town at the southern end of Van Diemen's Land, the ship's progress consistently frustrated by bad weather and contrary winds blowing up from the southwest.

'Who is Jesus Christ?' the captain, who was a keen Methodist, would ask Mathinna, as their sloop bobbed up and down with the remnants of the great swells that churned the seas beyond this or that safe harbour to wild white hells.

'The child of God, sir.'

'What was Jesus Christ for us?' the captain continued, determined the child would have the basic catechism mastered by the time she reached her destination.

'Our righteousness. Sir.'

She stumbled over the long word, such that it sounded like 'rage-in-us'. But the captain was satisfied and continued.

'What is the Devil?'

'The enemy of our souls, sir.'

'How does he wage war on our souls?'

'By making us give in to sinful desires.'

'What was Jesus made to do for us?'

'Take on our sins for us, sir. Why—'

'Who crucified Jesus Christ?'

'The Jews, sir. But why, sir, why Jesus, he good fella, why he have to sin if we no sin?'

'Who are the Jews?'

'The people of God, sir.'

If Mathinna wondered what sinful desires might be, or why the people of God might wish to kill the child of God, or if she saw it as obvious, having grown up ruled by the children of God, it was impossible to know, for having completed her task to the captain's satisfaction, she burst into chatter.

'And sir, sir, Napoleon he good fella, he teach me count to seven, teach me good, he know that first fella and all and the fella who made mountain and tree and stars. Yes, sir, he know. Jesus he bleed like a blackfella.'

'Who taught you Shakespeare?' asked the captain, suddenly suspicious.

'Napoleon,' said the child, who knew nothing of anything called Shakespeare.

Mathinna did not arrive in Hobart Town as she had intended to leave Flinders Island: her slight body clad in the skin of a white kangaroo hunted by her father. When the child burst into tears at the prospect of leaving her people, the Protector told her it was impossible to arrive at Government House dressed as a savage, but he relented on the matter of her favourite companion, a ringtailed albino possum she had tamed. It ran round her shoulders, nuzzled inside her grubby shift, and frequently dropped round turds like lead balls from a shot tower.

He let her keep the animal not out of sentimentality, but for fear that she might do something untoward if she were denied at least one small comfort. Of the children of Ham that had not perished, she was the brightest: high-spirited, admittedly, but the most advanced and, recalling her composure in the wake of her father's death, perhaps the one with the greatest possibility of redemption.

But he took several months agreeing to the Franklins' request, citing weather and the child's health, and even advancing contrived pedagogical arguments. The real reason for the delay was that the child went missing every time she was about to be shipped out. And deep inside, Robinson grew oddly troubled, and it somehow made him feel a little better about himself when she was not able to be found. For there was about Sir John something that Robinson, ever a keen student and petitioner of power, could not quite put into words. He turned to prayer and

Scripture, in which he found not answers but the evasion of transcendence.

At the point his own prevarications ran too thin to be sustained, Mathinna intensified her own campaign to stay by absconding with two native women to a sealers' colony on Gun Carriage Island. If the Protector was loath to part with that for which the Franklins asked, if he was failing to find Mathinna, he was nevertheless succeeding in persuading himself that he would hardly be abandoning the child to the scum of the penal colony. Rather, he told himself, it was to the very finest flowers of England, disciplined in habit, religious in thought, scientific in outlook—a woman who seemed to be the worthy consort of a man celebrated as one of the greatest names in the annals of heroic endurance, and that man himself. And their selfless goal? To raise the savage child to the level of a civilised Englishwoman. How could he deny anyone such opportunity?

Finally he had locked Mathinna in a room in his own house for a week, confiscated her possum and refused to give it back until she was embarked on a small sealing sloop, the *Cormorant*. He gave her some ship's biscuits as a parting gift, but he had not stayed to farewell her, instead returning to his house to read Scripture until dusk fell and the boat was lost to sight.

The *Cormorant* had fallen so far behind schedule that the captain offloaded his cargo for Hobart at a small inlet at the head of the Derwent estuary. There he came to an arrangement with a silver-haired old sawyer carting firewood. At first, the sawyer hadn't wanted anything to do with the black child. His brother, a convict shepherd, had been speared to death by blacks in a raid on his outstation during the Black War. But in exchange for some sealskins—the captain wished to hurry back to the islands to collect more—the sawyer finally agreed to take Mathinna through to Hobart Town.

The sawyer looked down at the small child and resolved she would be no more to him than a bag of chaff to be delivered. Though only a blue tattoo of her name remained on his shoulder, he had once had a daughter. He noticed a lump in the girl's smock, and dangling out below a button at waist level was a tail. He leant down, tugged the tail as he might a door pull, and was surprised when two large and sleepy pink eyes and a damp nose poked out.

With hands that were at once very large and very gentle, that seemed like a sea eagle's nest made of gnarled eucalypt branches, the sawyer picked up Mathinna. Holding the small weight and trust of the child in his grasp, he began to fear that hate was beyond him.

She looked up at the sawyer's face. One of his eyes was dead and milky, and his hair reminded her of a mat of bleached she-oak needles. As he slowly swung her through the air, she felt safe with the old man. He sat her down on the seat board of his cart, and then, in spite of his promise to himself, he found a dirty rug in the tray and spread it over her knees.

'Garney,' he said.

He noticed her bare feet poking out from the rug's

ragged bottom and, reaching down, he tweaked her big toe. He smiled.

'Garney Walch.'

The child had seen nothing like the town, a vast confusion of white men in many colours, and large buildings and mud and shit and horses—so many horses! And the whole effect, as she rode by the new warehouses and the older grog shops and slum cottages, as they drove past pigs and cows roaming free in the streets, men in yellow and black clothes chained like oxen, men in red clothes leaning on muskets, and finally up a hill to Government House, was one of overwhelming excitement.

A few people here and there stopped and pointed at her, shaking their heads as though they had seen a ghost.

'Why, Gunna?' she asked the sawyer, unable to pronounce his name.

'Well,' said Garney Walch, who didn't have an answer he wanted to tell the child, 'because . . . because you're going to be their new princess, that's why.'

When they arrived at her new home, they were directed around the back to a bustling series of outbuildings that served as kitchen, abattoir, laundry, stables, piggery and servants' quarters to the large house.

'Don't leave me,' she said, as he picked her up off the seat board.

'These are good people,' he said. But when he went to put her down, she dug her hands and feet into him and the possum ran round the back of his neck. 'The best people,' he said.

He didn't believe it. Nor did she. She clung to him ever harder.

'Don't go,' she said. Her bony frame was that of a terrified bird, pushing in and out against his old body. And though he wanted to hold and soothe what had nothing to do with him, he had to tear her and the possum off him and give them both to a small woman with a birthmark over fully half her face, soft and strange as an overripe apricot.

Garney Walch left quickly, cursing himself for feeling as bad as he did, his soul painfully open to a wound he thought long ago healed.

The woman bathed Mathinna in a wooden trough that ran along one side of the brick-nogged stables and out of which horses drank. The water was cold, the mountain covered in snow, and the black child irritated the convict maid with her silence.

After, the maid took her into the kitchen and fed her some tripe and potatoes. The food calmed the girl. As her fear began to subside, she sensed an inner life to the house that propelled all the energy, the resentment, the strange furtive gestures and quick asides, the groans and the odd laughter; the way, amazing to her and so unlike Wybalenna, that people never seemed to halt and sit and talk but kept on at their tasks like ants.

Mathinna was taken to her rooms. The first room, though not wallpapered, was freshly distempered and austerely furnished with a desk and stool, an easel and a small bookcase of primers and grammars to occupy her idle moments. For, as Lady Jane told several dinners in a row until even Sir John grew weary of it and asked her to talk about something else, the child was about to embark on a rigid programme of improvement. No moment was to be wasted, and all reckless passions were to be subjugated to the discipline of industry.

The second room was a corner room; the western windows faced onto the great timbered mountain range that was the backdrop for the town. Lady Jane, worried about the return of any painful nostalgia for a life in the woods, which she had heard afflicted all the natives incarcerated on Flinders Island, had ordered all the western windows' shutters to be nailed closed, leaving open only the northern window that looked out onto the industrious and elevating sight of the kitchen garden.

This was Mathinna's bedroom and contained within it what she thought was a third room—an intricate affair of coloured sails and wooden posts, so forbidding and mysterious that she mistook it for some whitefellas' tent that she was forbidden to enter. Only after the apricot-faced woman sighed, climbed up into the confusion of cotton and chintz and timber, and demonstrated its purpose by lying in its deep downy recesses, from where she said one simple word—'Bed'—did Mathinna finally understand its purpose. Leaping on it, she played there with the possum until, later that afternoon, the fruit-faced servant returned to find them lost in its folds, the black girl and the white possum, both asleep.

———

'Where are her shoes?' asked Lady Jane the following morning, when Mathinna was taken by her governess, the Widow Munro, to meet her new mother. For though the Aboriginal child was dressed in a dark grey serge dress of a type that attracts the word sensible, poking out from beneath its hem were two large, splayed and very brown feet.

'Don't talk to me about shoes!' said the governess. 'Shoes! May as well ask a snake why it won't get back in its skin.'

Lady Jane's aversion to snakes bordered on a phobia. But this was her very first meeting with the Aboriginal child as her new mother, and she had stressed to Sir John how important it was to establish the nature of their respective positions from the beginning. And so, much as she felt a sudden urge to pick the child up, she tried to regain her composure by returning to her intended comments.

'I am a modern in these matters,' said Lady Jane. 'Dress. Morals. The soul starts with detail and ends with tone.'

'Curtsy to the lady,' said the governess, who, while appearing a cicada husk of a woman, still delivered a shove in Mathinna's back worthy of a bullock driver.

'Man has judgement,' said Lady Jane, trying to ignore the governess, 'but woman sensibility.' The black child standing in front of her seemed as mysterious as a lynx from Siberia or a jaguar from the New World. 'But sensibility unrefined by moral improvement and mental discipline quickly declines into sensuousness, and sensuousness into wickedness. Do you understand me?'

Mathinna understood none of it and said nothing.

'You were given them, Mathinna? Shoes—you were given some good boots or some such?'

'She arrived with a wild beast and worse insolence,' said the governess. 'Impossible enough to get her body fully covered and half-respectable, far less her feet shod.'

Women were thin on the ground in the convict colony, and governesses almost unknown, so the discovery of the Widow Munro, formerly the wife of an officer of the Rum Corps, had at first seemed to Lady Jane a godsend. But it wasn't turning out at all well. Lady Jane pressed on.

'The programme I have devised for you stresses woman's natural virtues of faith, simplicity, goodness, self-sacrifice, tenderness and modesty.' How she longed to hold the child.

'They like it, they say,' said the Widow Munro. 'The dust and the mud and the earth hot and cold.'

Mathinna looked at the floor. A flea leapt from her hair to Lady Jane's wrist.

'You will be taught reading and spelling, grammar, arithmetic—'

'That's why,' interrupted the Widow Munro, 'they don't take to the shoeing.'

'She will be shod and she will be civilised,' said Lady Jane to the Widow Munro, forcing a smile. 'And I trust you to ensure that both things happen. Now, Mathinna. Where were—'

'Arithmetic,' said the Widow Munro.

'Yes,' continued Lady Jane, 'and geography, then you will move on to more elevated subjects such as . . .'

How, as she went on with her dreary litany, Lady Jane wanted to dress that little girl up and tie ribbons in her hair, make her giggle and give her surprises and coo lullabies in her ear. But such frivolities, she knew, would only ruin the experiment and the young child's chances. Mathinná would one day recognise the wisdom of her benefactress. For such lapses ran risks that Lady Jane did not even dare think about: risks of the heart that might confuse her; risks of the soul that might undo her. And knowing she wouldn't—that she mustn't—she went on listing the subjects Mathinna was to study.

'. . . rhetoric and ethics, as well as music, drawing and needlework. Catechism shall be our—'

'My lady,' the Widow Munro burst out in exasperation, 'the child is little more than a savage. A pleasant savage, I will admit—'

'I have a great belief in education,' said Lady Jane, fixing the Widow Munro with her most forbidding stare.

'I know my business,' said the Widow Munro, who, with the eternal belief in her own method, was in this, if nothing else, a true pedagogue and not easily swayed by the arguments of the ignorant outside her trade. 'They have thicker skulls. I have a manual on the instruction of the feeble-minded I will—'

'You will do no such thing,' said Lady Jane, seeming to emphasise her point with a loud slap of her right hand on her left forearm, but rather seeking to squash whatever had just bitten her. 'She will be treated as a free-born Englishwoman because that, too, is part of my experiment.'

Lady Jane dismissed them both. Harsh and distant as it seemed, she told herself that what she was doing was so much better for the child than holding her. She cursed herself. She could not believe her own lie, her cruel crushing of her own desire, yet believe it she would.

'One last thing, Mrs Munro,' said Lady Jane as the Widow approached the door. 'She will be shod or you shall be gone.'

For the first year, cobbler after cobbler made the trip to Government House with their tapes and their lasts and their leather as Lady Jane persisted in having new shoes made for Mathinna. And for the first year she had, under the combination of threats and inducements, out of a lonely child's desperate desire to please and not offend, worn the beautiful court shoes and party shoes, the ankle-high kid-skin boots. But her feet hurt. Wearing shoes, she felt as if her body had been blindfolded.

But she wanted to write and Lady Jane said she could have pen and ink and paper only if she kept her shoes on. For the magic of written words had not escaped Mathinna. She had watched Sir John and Lady Jane pore over the scratchings, like so many plover tracks in the sand, that marked the boxes of bound paper they read. Large currents of feeling passed through them. After, they would laugh or grimace or seem to be dreaming. She listened to the music of the scratchings when Lady Jane read poetry out loud, and saw the power of them to affect others when

Sir John looked up from his silent reading of memoranda and ordered a lackey to act. Their meaning was large and often unexpected.

'Is God the Father writing me?' Mathinna excitedly asked Lady Jane, when, on going to the beach at Sandy Bay for a picnic, she had seen seagull tracks in the sand, thinking perhaps Towterer was sending her some message. Lady Jane had laughed, and Mathinna realised that what was written in the world mattered not, but what was written on paper mattered immensely.

She wanted to write and so she agreed to the blindfold of shoes. She tried to feel her way through this strange world with her other senses—stumbling, falling, ever unsure—all in order to learn a little of the white magic of paper and ink.

Sometimes, as she lay alone in those two large rooms that were hers, so alone in an emptiness that felt to her greater than the starry night, she tried to unravel her many fathers. It was like the catechism: it made sense if you repeated it enough and didn't ask questions. There was God her Father, and Jesus his Son, who was also a sort of a father; there was the Protector, who had the Spirit of God the Father; and then there was Sir John, who was also her father, her new father—so many fathers.

But she was writing not to them, but to King Romeo, whom the old people called Towterer, who had gone to where all the old people go, that place of the hunt and the forests, a world from which no one returned. And she knew the magic of white paper would reach him there and he would understand all that she was trying to tell him: her loneliness, her dreams, her wonder, her joy, her ongoing ache of sadness—all the things that were in danger of vanishing.

'*Dear Father,*' she wrote.

> *I am good little girl. I do love my father. I have got a doll and shift and a petticoat. I read books not birds. My father I thank thee for sleep. Come here to se mee my father. I thank thee for food. I have got sore feet and shoes and stockings and I am very glad. All great ships. Tell my father two rooms. I thank thee for charity. Please sir please come back from the hunt. I am here yrs daughter*
> *MATHINNA*

Lady Jane was encouraged by the letter.

'Wisely,' she told Mrs Lord, a common and vulgar woman said to have used her charms to advance to her position as first lady of the free settlers, 'we removed her from the pernicious influence of the dying elements of her race, then introduced her to the most modern education an Englishwoman can receive. And,' she could not stop herself adding, 'the results are surprising all.'

But when Towterer failed to come to her or even reply—not after her first or second or even third letter—Mathinna's passion for writing began to fade and she was reminded of how much her feet hurt. And when she discovered her letters stashed in a pale wooden box beneath a skull, she felt not the pain of a deceit for which she had no template, but the melancholy of disillusionment. Writing and reading, she realised, did not exist magically beyond people, but were simply another part of them.

Thereafter she contemplated the lessons of the Widow Munro as she did the thrashings she routinely received at her hand—like being caught in a storm: better avoided, but beyond judgement or anguish. And she seemed to find in her endless punishments cause only for learning something deeper and darker than the grammatical constructions and theological precepts to which she had become utterly oblivious, and her success at which she was now uncaring. One day, she set down her sampler, the bare trunk of the tree of knowledge, took off her court shoes, and walked outside.

Lady Jane discovered Mathinna playing barefoot in the garden with a sulphur-crested cockatoo she had caught and tamed. This would have been punishable but excusable. Her crime paled when compared to that of the Widow Munro, who was found open-mouthed and foul-gummed drinking gin and sugar in the kitchen with the cook.

The search for a tutor began again and turned up several short-lived successors. There was the one-time poisoner Joseph Pinguid. He arrived in a rattly trap on which a wicker chair was improbably secured by old rope, and on top of which he—a plump, red-whiskered man in ragged Wellington boots several sizes too large—was even more impossibly perched. He was undone by the same contrivance: mounting his trap to depart Government House after the first day's lessons, an oversized Wellington slipped, he seized the chair to keep balance and the chair broke free of the tray. As old wicker and new tutor fell heavily to the ground, there tumbled out of Joseph Pinguid's overstuffed devil-skin satchel a silver platter bearing the Franklin crest.

There followed Karl Grolz, a Viennese music master, whose abilities were limited to the viola, and then the machine breaker Peter Hay, whose Owenite thinking and endless references to Fourier and Saint-Simon revealed him as one whose thinking was possibly limited by nothing. All went quickly; none made much of an impression, except to further tarnish a project that was already regarded by much of Van Diemonian society with disdain, if not outright contempt. Had not Mrs Lord asked if Mathinna was to be Lady Jane's pageboy?

'As though the child were a Gibraltar monkey,' raged Lady Jane to her husband. 'Just some exotic ornament to our vanity.'

Abandoning any hope of finding what she sought in Van Diemen's Land, Lady Jane, through an acquaintance in New South Wales, secured a new tutor from Sydney, who arrived by boat on a hot March morning two months later. Mr Francis Lazaretto was six feet four, a long, lean man with a shock of white hair that bristled over his angular face like a distemper brush. He wore a coat that may once have been dashing but was now as weary as he, patched with bits of grubby flannel. He was a man so funereal in appearance that Sir John found himself calling for a glass of brandy to help him recover after their first meeting, an act out of keeping with both his character and the early time of day.

'My God, you wouldn't even employ him as a tombstone,' said Sir John, throwing the glass down in a single gulp.

But, as Lady Jane pointed out, on an island at the end of the world where trees shed bark instead of leaves, where birds bigger than humans roamed, and where they were charged with turning a cesspit into a perfumery, they had to make do with what was on offer.

'If the potter's hand has slipped with the clay he shaped for us,' she said, 'we have no choice but to drink as best we can from his misshapen vessels.'

Unburdened by children of her own, Lady Jane had the strongest and most unbending ideas on the nature and necessity of education for the children of others. In Francis Lazaretto she was delighted to meet a mirror who simply reflected back a reverse image of her own strong opinions. His morbid appearance, she now saw, was but a mask for an unexpected intensity.

In a former life Francis Lazaretto had failed in his ambition to become a pantomime actor, but his long study of the genius of nonsense had not been without some good effect. He dared engage Lady Jane in a pedagogical argument by seizing a copy of Rousseau's *Émile* from her bookshelf and waving it about in support of his contention that Lady Jane's ideas would create a young woman profoundly unsuited to the modern world. If nothing else, he understood the value, properly used and convincingly displayed, of a good prop.

'The authorities concur,' said Francis Lazaretto, now

brandishing that most famous argument for modern education as an exorcist might the good book, 'that a distinction must always be observed: a woman is educated to be governed; while your suggestions would create an absurdity—a woman like a man, self-governing.'

While this seemed to Lady Jane a distinction with which she disagreed, it proved to her the inestimable worth of Francis Lazaretto. What in another she might have found almost manic, was in him mesmerising.

'Nine-tenths of what we are, Mr Lazaretto, good or evil, useful or useless, comes, does it not, you would agree, from our education?'

Francis Lazaretto, who had produced a forged letter from the Master of Magdalen College proving conclusively he had passed two years at Oxford reflecting on the classics, had instead known education for only four years as limited rote-learning and almost limitless violence in a Yorkshire boarding school of dubious intent. In consequence, he understood his own achievements as very much his own, and he did not agree at all. What self-made man would? But what self-made man on the make ever disagreed with a superior beyond what was necessary to establish himself as a creature of worth and independence?

'Of course, Ma'am,' he replied.

Feeling he had through opposition sufficiently established his bona fides, Francis Lazaretto put down both Rousseau and his own opinion, and introduced St Thomas Aquinas in support of Lady Jane's arguments and in contradiction of his own, quoting the great ecclesiastical authority as declaring that all men are, at first, a clean tablet on which nothing is written.

'Precisely,' said Lady Jane, pleased to discover the immortals had also been persuaded by her convictions. 'The distance between savagery and civilisation is measured by our control of our basest instincts. And the road travelled to civilisation is, I intend to show, enlightened education.'

Sir John was less sure about what he termed Francis Lazaretto's 'insinuating midshipman's air', but Lady Jane understood her husband's lack of enthusiasm as the jealousy of a man untutored in these great debates.

'On this forsaken prison-island, we have had the good fortune to find the one man who understands the gravity and necessity of our experiment,' she told him, as a convict footman lit a fire of cow dung in the coal grate to keep at bay the mosquitos. Above all else, it was her husband's thinning hair that annoyed her, the white wisps of which reminded her of a spider's web—and revolted her because in them she intimated her own approaching age, and with it the vile cage in which all old women were put. Sir John kept the wisps plastered over his dome with a black pomade that on hot days left his brow criss-crossed with greasy dark streaks.

'God could not have been kinder,' she said coldly.

Seeing the reformation of a savage as a moment when his personal destiny—hitherto sorrowful, following his transportation after a shop-keeper swore false witness against him—might be forever after linked with that of the nobler histories of Science and Christianity,

Francis Lazaretto at first approached his task with sincere industry, devising a complete syllabus of Latin, Greek and rhetoric, each day beginning and ending with a thorough study of the Scriptures. In accordance with the most modern thinking, while literacy was stressed to the utmost, frivolities such as novels were banned and a wide variety of moral grammars imported from Sydney for Mathinna's edification.

Lady Jane was publicly delighted and privately intimidated by Francis Lazaretto's programme, which he presented in a carefully tabulated chap book, with each left-hand page of columns accounting for another week of lessons, prayer, marks and attitude, and each right-hand page blank in order that he could record there his observations of Mathinna's progress, for which the programme admitted no possibility of alteration, far less failure.

'It would break me,' said Sir John, but on seeing his wife's thin lips purse, quickly mumbled, 'but a child is a *tabula rasa*, not an old moth-eaten book.'

The room designated as the schoolroom faced the harbour and had large windows to aid reading. Yet they always seemed to draw Francis Lazaretto to look at the world outside and the brilliant sun spilling off the sea beyond. For he was given to manias, and weather seemed to set them off—hot weather leaving him euphoric and cold weather conducive only to melancholy. It had been hot when he had met the Governor and his wife, but then the weather changed and the mountain grew iron-grey with snow cloud as Lady Jane's grand experiment finally got properly underway.

And as the sun on the water vanished, as the water turned to ruffled lead, Francis Lazaretto found he had no heart for any of it. It was, he realised, pointless. Pointless and meaningless, as he felt almost everything in his life to be.

His second week began and Francis Lazaretto wept not long after. He sat and stared at the grey cloud. The child seemed to understand when he talked to her of his pain. She understood many things, he came to realise, and he told her about his life and the women he had known, and the way all *that* was also meaningless and pointless. She taught him a dance, which she said was that of the echidna, along with several words of her native tongue.

In his third week of tutoring, the clouds melted and his mood improved markedly; the need to instil Latin declensions and Greek conjugations reasserted itself, but it was all too late. Mathinna had warmed to her tutor, and the tutor's concerns seemed to have altered considerably. Lady Jane walked in one day to find them both playing with Mathinna's parrot: they had devised a form of football in which the bird and they competed for a walnut that the bird rolled with its beak.

'Mr Lazaretto no Mr Lazaretto at all,' said Mathinna after the second month. 'He Jesus Christ and he been sent among us to—'

'He is what?'

'He the saviour, Ma'am,' said Mathinna, who had found Mr Lazaretto's catechism more extraordinary and certainly more entertaining than any she had ever heard. 'Of us all. He say others do not see it, like they do not see the snakes flying over Hobart Town of a night and the bats under our feet of a day. He say as God was unknown to me, so he unknown to the whitefellas, but this will change come next Easter, Miss.'

It transpired that Francis Lazaretto had never been a tutor, though he had once worked as a dancing master. Apart from acting, he had no aptitude for anything much beyond playing ditties on a button accordion and a certain dexterity at Aunt Sally, a game he taught Mathinna, in which they competed to knock down a set of skittles by lobbing long staves.

Lady Jane did not accept that her failure with Mathinna disproved her theories—rather it demonstrated powerfully their rightness: clearly too much had transpired by the age of seven, and what must happen was the breaking of all bonds from birth. Only in this way would change for the better be possible. What was clearly needed, she now told Sir John, was the building of a world that would shape the earliest impressions favourably—from birth children must breathe in the fresh air of civilisation, not the stinking miasma of forests.

The design for the glyptotech having arrived, Lady Jane purchased some hundreds of acres to the northwest of Hobart in Kangaroo Valley, where she intended to build her temple to the arts. It would help regenerate the empty and frivolous of the colony, she told Sir John; it would be an area conducive to the study of natural history; and it would show how art, properly understood and in its most classical expression, as represented in twenty-four plaster of Paris reproductions, could help the soul advance from primitive passion to civilised reason. In this way, Lady Jane's plans for Mathinna's advancement were never completely abandoned, but were used as an argument for new projects.

So it was that the child, who was unobtrusive and charming, grew up avoiding her lessons, Francis Lazaretto and she having arrived at a perfectly acceptable arrangement that saw them pass the morning together playing and left her afternoons free to do whatever she wished. Late one summer afternoon, when Sir John had gone into the Government House gardens with Montague to take some air, he looked up from a conversation about a new wharf that was not going well to see the Aboriginal girl in a red dress.

Though, on arriving in Hobart, she had soon acquired an extensive wardrobe of cuts and colours, Mathinna's inevitable preference was for red. Nothing had caught her fancy like the red dress that Lady Jane had herself worn as a child, and which she had given Mathinna as a present on the first anniversary of her arrival. Button-shouldered and short-sleeved, belted with a black velvet band, the red dress was made of the lightest silk and cut in the simple high-waisted style popular in the wake of the French Revolution, when anything more elaborate was deemed aristocratic decadence.

Mathinna was at the far end of the main gravel path, playing with her cockatoo, sprinkling water over its awkwardly outstretched wings as it strutted around a fountain like an old drunk. As the bird waddled, Mathinna danced, a strange dance, where at times her own body seemed to be floating. As they came closer, Sir John realised that she was singing in her own strange yet strangely incantatory tongue.

Until that day he hadn't really noticed Mathinna, viewing her as one more in a very long series of his wife's enthusiasms, best endured like wind and snow, silently and stoically. That day, though, he saw her as if for the first time. Only now, as they walked towards her, did Sir John notice her eyes, which so many others had commented on. They seemed the largest and darkest eyes imaginable. And though only very occasionally and only after considerable encouragement and admonition could they be properly glimpsed, he understood why they were so much admired. She had learnt the odd art of playing the coquette, which she regarded as simply a different animal dance.

Only now, as they continued on past her, did Sir John finally realise she was, as Montague put it admiringly—and he was from the beginning anything but an admirer—the most beautiful savage he had ever seen. But it wasn't her looks—neither Nubian nor of the Levant, but something else again—that first enchanted Sir John. It was the way she smiled at him.

It was true, as he told Lady Jane over dinner, that it was 'the contrast of that wild beauty with the civilised dress of the Age of Reason' he found delightful, but it was the sudden, unexpected flashing gleam of teeth that disarmed him. Gleam of teeth, swirl of red, puddle of eye, dance of feet. Sir John had been everywhere—but he had never seen anything like her. He felt as if he had just awoken.

On the day the glyptotech opened, Lady Jane looked up at the wild mountain, its snowy peak lost in mist, and then back at the sandstone Greek temple that now sat at the head of that picturesque forested valley. Once, perhaps, she thought, Zeus did sport here, transforming into whatever animal he needed to be—a bull, a goat, a swan—in order to take yet another mortal or goddess unawares. At that moment a kangaroo came bounding across the temple. As its rising and falling body linked the Corinthian columns at the front of the temple with sweeping arcs of flight, Lady Jane laughed at her absurd fantasy.

Mathinna stood with Lady Jane and the official party, but her status was changing. Less and less was she the Franklins' adopted daughter, and more and more was she some other creature whom they came to regard as they did several other pets around Government House—the albino possum, her cockatoo, a wombat—an exotic object of amusement.

Sir John had begun to seek Mathinna out and have her sing songs in her native tongue; then, as he got to know her better, he had her dance the kangaroo dance and the possum dance, the echidna dance and the emu dance, but the one he particularly enjoyed was the black swan dance, in which she would jack-knife her body backward and jolt her arms forward and out, as if rising into flight.

Those who wished to enter the Franklins' circle had to acknowledge Mathinna, had to profess themselves amused and charmed by the black girl. She took pleasure in her status, demanding curtsies from all, and she now castigated the servants, whom she had once been too shy even to look in the eye, for not satisfying her whims.

And when, that day of the opening of Ancanthe, as the glyptotech was named, Mathinna's cockatoo flew onto Montague's shoulder and left a wet, white dropping trailing down his black coat, not even Sir John's assurance that such things were good luck could drown out the laughter of the black girl, so raucous and uninhibited that it infected the whole party until they were all laughing.

A humiliated Montague whispered to his wife that the child behaved not like a lady, but some wild thing. And he pointed to the ground, where they could see her naked toes forking their way in and out of the mud.

'Like filthy grubs and worms,' sneered Montague. 'It is as if dirt itself were a pleasure.'

The more Mathinna stopped being what the Franklins expected and the more she became herself, the more the Governor grew to like her. He was fascinated by 'the forest sprite', as he called her, both because of her general liveliness and her particular ability to appear out of nowhere and startle people: none more so than Lady Jane, who found it a trait at first amusing, then slightly disturbing and finally immensely irritating—for what exactly had the child heard, and what had she seen? And what did she know, what did she think, that smiling black enigma?

Lady Jane would feel something wrapping around her and look down to see black arms around her waist. She would twist and stride off, and Mathinna, sensing it was a game, would take two skips to join her and, with a cry of glee, again wrap her arms around Lady Jane's legs. Lady Jane could smell her then, that wild, dangerous, dog smell of children. Once more she would push the child away, yet still Mathinna would persist and reach out, seeking to grab one of Lady Jane's skirt-clad thighs.

'Please, Mathinna,' Lady Jane would say softly, grabbing her wrist harshly. '*Please.* I don't like that.'

Nor, said Sir John, did he. But secretly he began to crave such touch and warmth. He loved the way Mathinna moved, so quick and alive. He watched entranced as, one afternoon, she made traps for the seagulls that plagued the port town—a simple affair of a piece of bread at the end of a long string, which with infinite patience she drew towards a cairn made of twisted branches and bark, behind which she waited and, when the moment was right, grabbed the bird in a single lightning-like movement. He spent the rest of the day playing this game with her, ignoring Montague's occasional interruptions that he was late for this appointment or that meeting, until he finally managed to draw the seagull into the trap; but he was so slow lunging after it that the bird was in flight and Mathinna laughing before he had finished falling.

Sir John could not forget that laugh. Under his breath he boxed the compass, reciting in perfect order the sailors' catechism: 'North—North by east—Northeast by north', the thirty-two points of order that summoned home's certainty out of an oceanic emptiness. 'Northeast—Northeast by east—East-northeast,' he would mumble to forget that laughter's enticing sound.

But he was south of no north now, and every compass point served only to concentrate his thoughts more powerfully upon her. For whether it was west by northwest or south-southeast, she was everywhere. And when he resorted to naming the winds and their origins, still it did no good, for Lady Jane had insisted that Mathinna should have a bell tied around her wrist so that they might know where she was, so that her presence would not frighten Lady Jane or the various dignitaries visiting Government House, and to ensure that the 'empty black vessel', as Lady Jane began calling her, 'will not fill with any more indiscretions'. And just naming the Sirocco of the Southeast or the Mistral of the Northwest was enough to bring to Sir John's ears the sound of that tinkling.

'Can they not see,' hissed Montague to his wife, 'that the child *is* the indiscretion?'

It wasn't long before Sir John's new interest in his adopted daughter began to affect his work. He found himself increasingly fed up with the daily tedium of executive council meetings in the morning, the endless wearying interviews with countless supplicants after lunch, the minutes to be signed, the memoranda to be dictated, the orders and inspections and enquiries—to say nothing of the social dreariness of night after night of dining with people he now found the dullest in the world, none of whom he could ever imagine having the wit or agility to catch a seagull, all of whom were determined not to reveal a single human emotion in front of the man who, for all intents and purposes, was their king. He completed his tasks, but his once implacable attention to detail was gone. He was beginning to live in two worlds, and only one mattered to him.

With Mathinna, Sir John played Aunt Sally, he rolled the walnut with the cockatoo and joined in the songs she had been taught by Francis Lazaretto. With her was possible all that wasn't as Governor, things that were common and simple and fun, in which he could say something foolish or innocent—or, as he frequently did, both—and suffer no consequence. With the Aboriginal child he felt he could be himself.

There were other effects, though. Even he was alarmed at how he was becoming softer, more aware of the sufferings and wants of others, and this led him to several acts of compassion that were interpreted as folly and, worse, weakness. He pardoned the five convicts who had for two years cut the track over which he and Lady Jane travelled through the southwest. He sought to limit the use of the lash.

'The man has no understanding of power,' Montague

confided to Chief Justice Pedder, as he shuffled the cards in preparation for their weekly game of piquet.

Unused to joy and seeking to justify it as duty, Sir John told himself, as he took to telling others, that this was a most singularly important experiment for the colony's future. But not the least attractive aspect of Mathinna for Sir John was that when he was with her, he couldn't give a fig for the experiment, the colony or its future. Secretly he delighted in what had become his life: those few stolen moments with the child, as opposed to the interminable fantasy world of colonial government, which he increasingly lived in only as a shell. Because he no longer had opinion or ambition or interest, and because his wife had all these things, he abdicated all responsibility and even took to openly asking her advice and immediately endorsing it, without either discussion or enthusiasm, while his ear was ever waiting only for the tinkling of Mathinna's wrist.

'Why have you allowed this?' asked Montague, disturbed at the way the Governor now gave his enemies all the evidence they needed.

'Why not?' replied Sir John. And he laughed, because out of the window he could see Mathinna playing with her possum, which, with its large eyes for seeing better in its preferred night-time wanderings, wore the same look of astonished amusement as Montague at that moment.

Sir John had inherited his secretary from his predecessor, Arthur. In the troubled history of the colony, with its outbreaks of banditti and black wars, the savagery of the slavery of the convicts, the mythical stories of men who ate each other and the determination of his predecessor to hang as many men as was necessary—in order that all would understand that they could hope for anything except hope itself—Montague had played a quiet but essential role. He understood power as the dominion of necessity, not as a justification to go on *en plein air* watercolour painting expeditions. He despised the Franklins above all else for their naiveté.

'Someone has to,' continued Sir John, 'and my wife wants to.' And he laughed again, because he understood that Montague could not see how trivial and pointless ruling anything or anybody was. Sir John knew he was being careless, but his contempt was so complete he did not think it could be of any consequence.

'Power is like that too,' Chief Justice Pedder said to Montague, after the latter had recounted this story. 'It is the kingdom of forgetting.' He declared a retique, took sixty points and won the game.

Still, on occasion Sir John felt ashamed of himself and, as a pious man, asked God in his prayers for His guiding wisdom. He felt he was what he knew the colonists increasingly whispered: a useless fat old man infatuated with a piccaninny. He tried to focus his thoughts on anything but the Aboriginal child. But only the memory of her laugh and easy movements restored in him any sense of youth and purpose. No one more than Sir John himself was struck by the enigma that was his life. And when he met Mathinna the next morning, he told her more stories of the great polar lands, tales of endless ice and frozen worlds, while inside, his heart was scalded all over again by the most sinful desire.

'But you can only keep power,' Montague said to Chief Justice Pedder, laying down his cards and handing over to Pedder a proposal for several new penal reforms which Sir John had that morning announced he wished to see enacted, 'if you forgive nothing and remember everything.' The proposal was written in Lady Jane's hand. And both men, who had survived the pestilential intrigues of a prison yard become a society and kept their power for a long time, read the document carefully, for both men fully intended to continue to survive and keep power for a longer time yet.

Sir John could not help it. Nor could he help himself. That smile, that laugh, that way of pulling at his arm to gain attention, tugging at his trouser leg, leaning and rolling against him as if he were a rubbing post, that way of—he shuddered with the memory. So many sensations, too many memories—all innocent, of course—but something led him to put them out of his mind. It was her touch, he thought with a shock as abrupt as the sensation of her fingers, her hand. Her body touching his.

Above all, she loved toasted cheese. Sir John would have buttered toast and toasted cheese prepared for her, and then would watch her greedy little mouth intently as the yellow fat oiled her hungry lips. Once sated, she would immediately look for her parrot with which to play—or, failing to find the bird, for Sir John to come with her, which invariably he would, faithful as a puppy, timid as a possum and certainly more tractable than a cockatoo, sometimes peeved, sometimes frustrated, but ever obedient.

Sometimes he snuck into her bedroom just to watch her sleep—so unlike Lady Jane, who seemed like an old wheezing dog in comparison with this angelic child who hardly emitted a whisper. He thrilled at seeing the dark down on her exposed forearm, and as he leant in with his candle, the better to see her, he would wish to kiss her eyes, her lips. But, terrified of his engorged heart, he would abruptly straighten and leave.

He was enchanted and, like all those enchanted, he wanted proximity to his enchantress, and he manoeuvred and manipulated to make sure he got it. If he thought there was a wrongness, even a perversity, in his growing infatuation, he gave no sign of it. Rather he advanced into it, had the whole of Government House enthuse about this marvellous experiment being conducted with such vigorous joy, implicated society by having them applaud Mathinna when she entered a room, had Hobart Town wave when she sat with him in the vice-regal carriage as they travelled through the city.

When it snowed he took her sledding on the lower slopes of the mountain where he had a passable run cleared by some convicts: how Mathinna squealed as she rode down on the sleigh he had specially built. When it shone he took her sailing on the expanse of the Derwent estuary, though this rather bored her. And when her possum went missing and she was inconsolable, he personally took toasted cheese to her rooms, and was mystified when she threw the plate at the wall. Mathinna never told him that when the animal had not returned from its nocturnal life to her bed at dawn, she had gone searching, only to find one of Montague's kangaroo dogs cracking a skinned possum carcass between its slobbery jaws.

She was given a wombat and a horse as consolation, and life rolled on. They picnicked, played Aunt Sally, and over Lady Jane's objection that it was irredeemably middle class, Sir John taught Mathinna cribbage rather than Lady Jane's preference, calabresella, a game for three, which she said was popular with the clergy of the Latin peninsula. He countered that if he were to teach a game it would be English.

But the game's nationality was meaningless to Mathinna. She simply loved the jumping dance of the stick markers up and down the crib board, calling it the kangaroo game. Over the leaping markers were to be heard burps, laughter, sighs, sneezes, giggles, groans and squeals. In time there were discussions, opinions and observations. Then came sulks, squabbles, silences, jealousies and battles of will, for which Sir John would seek to make amends with fruit mince pies, outings and more toasted cheese.

Mathinna seemed to grow up at some absurdly accelerated pace; by nine he noticed her budding beneath her virginal white-silk Regency dress with its high waist and low collar. By ten there was a swelling suggestion of breasts and, with it, a changed attitude—more knowing, more devious, he felt in his more frustrated moments, and also more attractive, as if the two were somehow related, as if a new coyness and a new confidence were the same, as though the new passion for privacy and the new desire for experience were somehow one, and he determined to be an indivisible part of that oneness.

Her body—so small compared to her large head—moved with such grace, as Sir John himself noted, like the native tiger-cat, sudden leaps and Russian ballet-like bounds, and in her physical naturalness she seemed complete, as if she were already fully formed, an adult at ten, as though there were little more life allowed her.

Lady Jane could not help it—the idea of having to travel to a ship on a damp and wave-splashed tender simply for an evening's entertainment irritated her. For while she liked the aura of adventure, the slightest disruption to her routine was only ever a source of annoyance. And so, whenever she embarked on any of her travels to new worlds, she always insisted on taking her old world with her. That was why she had taken her forty-eight hat boxes on her celebrated journey through the heart of south-western Van Diemen's Land, borne aloft through its unmapped jungles on a blackwood palanquin shouldered by four barefoot convicts; and it was why she was in no particular mood to take pleasure in the elaborate costume in which her husband now appeared before her, ready for the grand costume ball on the departing Antarctic expedition ships, the HMS *Erebus* and the HMS *Terror*.

For Sir John stood before her improbably dressed as a black swan.

She had found him uncommonly animated and altogether unbearable since the two ships had arrived the autumn before, en route to the southern polar regions. On the day of the ships' berthing, Sir John had visited them and, after the obligatory ceremonies and inspections, was taken to the chart room of the *Erebus*, which doubled as the officers' galley.

On a long narrow table, the furled charts, sextant, compass and battered pencil stubs, and the open bottle of his favourite drink, Madeira, awoke in him a long dormant desire to return to exploration. The two captains, Crozier and Ross, had been greatly pleased to meet the famed polar explorer, and Sir John in turn had been at once flattered and overjoyed at what he described as having his family with him—by which he meant the Royal Navy explorers, but which Lady Jane was soon to come to think was more an asylum for the socially maladroit. The three explorers had quickly struck up a seagoing camaraderie— the language, passions and boisterous midships slaps and shoves—all of which Lady Jane found excluding and exceedingly dull.

They toasted English valour and English genius, they drank to English discoveries still to come, with the unworded hope shared by all that they too might one day become part of such a glorious English history. As he drained his second glass of Madeira and soon after discovered himself on his fifth, Sir John felt unburdened. He thought of how he would love to leave the wretched colony, be rid of its poisonous politics, his wife's intense ambitions, and once more exist in the white emptiness of the polar regions, where the choices and demands were straightforward: to explore, to chart, to survive, to return. The cold, the hunger, the deaths, the risks—all of these seemed not cause for concern or fear, but points of pride, realities that only he and a select few had met and conquered.

And Crozier!

'Such a fine specimen of a man,' he later told Lady Jane. 'It is said he is the handsomest in the Royal Navy!' Sir John did not add that such physical grandeur made him feel at once awkward, fat and clumsy in his presence, but also buoyed—more manly, taller and braver than he felt when in the company of others. 'Many of the ladies think,' he added, with a confidential inhalation, 'that he takes after Byron.'

'Only if he traded tallness for talent,' sniffed Lady Jane, who found Crozier's height off-putting. Though he did exude a certain dull sensuality that reminded Lady Jane of sitting next to a wet hunting dog, she could see no sign of any vice on the empty face far above. Though she would never have admitted it, she had secretly always rather envied Byron his gift for dissipation. But that was beside the point. Crozier was, once spoken to, phenomenally dull.

It had hardly thrilled her, then, when what had been intended as a provisioning and repair stop of only a few weeks had lengthened into several, and then it was apparent that winter was upon them and the wolfhound would stay with them, for the expedition chose to winter in Hobart rather than risk their lives in the long Antarctic night.

The delay delighted Sir John, however. He arranged for Ross and Crozier and their crews a series of entertainments, travels, parties and scientific projects. He personally oversaw the provedoring of their ships to ensure the expedition was not cheated in quality or quantity, took the officers shooting for emu and kangaroo, built an observatory to help them with their celestial observations, had every facility of the colony laid open for their use and benefit. Other than Mathinna, the expeditioners were his great passion.

In return for such hospitality, Ross and Crozier, before their long-delayed departure the following spring, arranged a ball to be held on the *Erebus*. Impressed by the wondrous animals they had seen and shot, its theme was to be the bestiary.

But Sir John, standing in front of Lady Jane in his elaborate motley of wire and feathers, mask in hand, could see that he was far more excited about this ball than his wife. He attempted to cajole her into a better humour.

'Why, Napoleon himself had a bedhead made for Josephine out of a Van Diemonian black swan,' he said, but even as he was saying it, he realised that she was further annoyed by the trouble he had taken with the exquisite folly of his black feathered wings. Her own costume was infinitely simpler—a simplicity she felt more appropriate to their position. She would wear a small mask of a fox's face, which she had made for her many years before when visiting Venice.

'I had the vanity of thinking,' said Sir John, somewhat affronted, 'that it might amuse you. The workmanship is exquisite.'

He had found a tailor who combined the sensitivity of a Maison Verreaux taxidermist with the craft of the finest couturier: a convict transported for bestiality—a detail the Governor thought better not to bring to his wife's attention—who had created the dark wings in a half-opened spread, such that it seemed Sir John might at any moment take flight. The taxidermist had infused his creation not just with the delight of reaching the sky, but with an unmistakeable suggestion of pleasures that spoke more of the earth. The mighty black swan's great wings swept forward and out, as if seeking their first purchase of air, and it made Sir John's body—normally evocative only of ease—appear as though it were already tensing for a straightening, a moment of wondrous release.

'You look an utter fool,' said Lady Jane.

Both the *Terror* and *Erebus* were spectacularly decorated for the occasion. Seven hundred looking glasses, destined for use in exchange with any natives the explorers might meet in the south polar regions, were hung off the ships' sides so that the Chinese lanterns with which the deck and masts were lit reflected back and forth across the harbour.

Everyone was excited, everyone was saying the same thing over and over about what a ball it would be, and Mathinna, resplendent in her favourite red dress and a wallaby mask, made her way hand in hand with Sir John, who was sombrely attired in his naval uniform. His only concession now to the evening's theme was a small black swan mask, which Mathinna, to his annoyance, had tried to pull off and throw into the harbour.

They walked up the gangplank and on to the *Erebus*'s upper deck, which for that night was to be the ballroom, past the bush flowers and manfern fronds and the awkward lackeys in livery fitting too tight or too loose, the flunkeys who wanted whatever it was that Mathinna already had—a way of being at the centre of things. She did not know this, but she could feel it in the way all these men and women in their strange animal costumes—platypuses, griffins, centaurs, unicorns and wombats—leant down and tried to catch her attention, how they wanted her to acknowledge them, to say something, but she just smiled; smiling was what worked, smiling kept Sir John and Ma'am happy, smiling kept something between you and them. From the corner of her eye she could see others adjusting themselves, with a rustle here and a sigh there, in front of a large mirror at the landing that led up to the foredeck. Around her floated compliments, bitter asides, meaningless words.

'Our princess of the wilds!' sighed a wolf.

All week she had practised the quadrille.

'The sweetest savage!' said a bear.

Mathinna skipped her left foot back and out and in and lifted her right hand to present it to her partner, one-two-three-four, concentrating on remembering what the beginning of the dance required, five-six-seven, while continuing to walk on, smiling here, smiling there.

'What became of their beautiful villages, I can't say,' a tiger was saying. 'The cause of enlightenment swept them away too, I suppose.'

She understood nothing of what was being said above her, except that while her blackness marked her out as exceptional, it also made her in some way not just bad, but wrong. And that made no sense, because she could remember all the steps.

'We didn't come here for society and civilisation. We came here for what everyone who isn't a convict comes here for: money.'

The military band struck up, and the extraordinary event strangely reminded Mathinna of the campfire evenings at Wybalenna, and the excitement and wonder she now felt in her stomach seemed oddly familiar and welcome.

'I felt—for a long time, too—I felt that a good intention would always lead to a good act, and that the truth will take all before it. Well, I don't have to tell you such feelings don't last long in Van Diemen's Land.'

Though Mathinna understood almost nothing of it, she let it all flow in, all the smells and sights and voices, all the music, while trying to remember how to count beats and how many bars it was before you span back around. But she refused all invitations to dance. She told those who asked that she was waiting for the quadrille. That was the dance she had practised, that she loved—the others she knew a little, but not enough to take to the floor, where she was frightened she would look clumsy and foolish.

They danced a cotillion, then a waltz was called for, then a scotch reel. They jigged and skipped, and some but not many danced in the more modern, stately fashion, but still Mathinna refused all entreaties to step up onto that part of the deck designated as a dance floor and instead leant into the main mast, watching, feeling it all build within her, listening to the music, the snatches of conversation, her right foot turning this way and that in a coiled ropes' bight.

'Are we no longer Your Excellency but Zeus himself?' Mrs Lord's young daughter rather boldly asked when Sir John danced with her, and he jovially shook his swan mask, chins below his beak rippling out in laughter.

As the evening wore on, the dancing grew more animated and excited. Occasionally a voice from beyond drifted through the military band's ever more determined efforts, the increasingly frenzied sound of so many bodies moving, shoes sweeping. Mathinna was filling with the music, sensing at first the intense desire for communion carried in all the bodies on the dance floor, then only aware of her own body—its memory, its desire—filling to overflowing.

Finally, the bandmaster called the quadrille.

When Mathinna accepted Sir John's hand and went onto the dance floor with the three other couples, there was polite applause. She felt hot, her breathing was short, but the moment the music started she felt in the centre of the world. She was vaguely aware of expressions of surprise at her accomplishment at the dance, and her steps grew more assured. After the lead couple—Mrs Lord and Captain

Crozier—performed the next set of steps, Mathinna and Sir John and the other two couples repeated them. As the intensity built, Mathinna began to introduce slight variations in her footwork, which became faster, more daring.

Mrs Lord, proud of her own abilities, ceased with the simple steps she had been leading with, and led with a complicated sequence involving some rapid step-work. Captain Crozier looked shocked and, though a fair dancer, only just managed to stay with his partner. But the Aboriginal girl repeated Mrs Lord's steps perfectly, and then, to growing applause, went on to mesmerise everyone with variations on her footwork and body turns, and even Mrs Lord halted for a moment to laugh and clap.

Mathinna was now so excited and so free it was as if she were tumbling through clouds. It was as though she was approaching some truth of herself, and people were applauding her for it. Someone was saying that there were fewer than seventy of the original race left at Mr Robinson's settlement, but the boat was rising up through her, she could feel the wind lifting and dropping her. Her movements were no longer steps or skips or slides but something magical that had taken hold of her body.

In the midst of the dance's lively finale, Mathinna realised she was no longer holding Sir John's hands nor in step with anyone else, as she had so patiently practised, but was moving to something more fundamental and deep-rooted than a dance invented fifteen years before in Paris.

Her cheeks were fired, her body liberated, her mind had never felt so free of what she now knew was a strange fog that had lain upon it for as long as she could remember. And yet she did not sense the strange rupture she was making in the evening. Her eyes had never felt so sharp, so able to see and know everything—but she failed to notice the gasps, the shaking of heads, the angry and dark looks as on and on she span and now jumped, as she felt not the wax with which the oak deck had been prepared but the earth of Van Diemen's Land, as with two deft movements she kicked off her shoes and became a kangaroo absolutely still, except for its head, click-clicking around, then a stamp, two leaps, and she was flying.

Everyone had stopped dancing and all were staring. What on earth was the child doing? Who was this savage? Why was she still allowed to be on the dance floor?

The band stopped playing.

Lady Jane remembered once saying the child's body thought. But, she now wondered, looking on in shock as Mathinna danced some unknown barbarous rite, what on earth was it thinking now?

Mathinna felt as if she only had this one moment on the deck of that boat to explain who she was—but who that was, no one would ever know, not even she, for they were all closing in around her. She tried to keep dancing but someone was yelling and something was wrong, so terribly wrong; she felt dizzy, the boat was spinning faster and faster, and she was no longer leaping and flying but falling and falling, and hands were coming to her, white hands, hands in awful gloves like rags used to dress the dying—and was she dying? She was unsure of everything.

She wanted to ask but no words came, but she needed to know: was it Rowra?

Mathinna came out of a skipping slumber sensing a presence above her. She opened her eyes and was immediately terrified. Above her loomed the face of a giant black swan. She knew her life was over.

'*Rowra*,' Mathinna whispered.

After she collapsed, Crozier had carried the small child in his great arms down to his captain's cabin, a room only fractionally longer and wider than the cot in which he laid her to rest, and in which she had now woken.

'What?' said Sir John.

The child said not a word more.

Far away, the ball continued, the band played on.

He was all things and all things were him. Looking down on Mathinna, her diminutive body, her exposed black ankles, her dirty little feet, the suggestive valley of her red dress between her thin legs, Sir John felt thrilled.

And after, was thrilled no more.

8

ON A COLD MORNING, during the third day of rehearsals at the Haymarket, halfway through a scene in which Ellen Ternan, playing Rose Ebsworth, has been embraced by her grieving friend Clara Burnham, played by her sister Maria, Ellen abruptly stepped out of character and her sister's embrace, crying out:

'Please, Maisy, *careful*, or I'll end up wearing pigeon pie!'

It was the first moment of spontaneous performance Dickens had seen from Ellen Ternan, but it was also not part of the script. Though part of him was intrigued and amused, Dickens was weary and simply lost his temper.

'Damn you, Miss Ternan!' he said tersely, holding up the script as if it were holy writ. 'We have ten days left—what are you doing?'

In answer, and not without hesitation, she reached inside her coat and produced a small glossy black bird. It oinked.

'They are great mimics, sir,' said Ellen Ternan, unsure of what else to say, holding the bird in her cupped hands as though it were some sort of offering.

'She's always collecting dying birds and trying to save them,' said Maria. 'She picked up this starling at the entrance of the Haymarket.'

'Its wing seemed a bit broken, Mr Dickens,' said Ellen Ternan. 'And I thought I must keep him warm.'

'A *bit*?' said Dickens. 'Well, we must be grateful it is not a lot.'

He reached down into the now quiet ball of shiny fluff that she held before him.

'I'll have a starling,' he said softly, retreating into recitation while pushing a finger first under one wing, then the other, slowly unfolding each in turn and inspecting the bird. 'It shall be taught to speak nothing but "Mortimer", and—'

Dickens looked up from the starling and for the first time looked into her eyes. He was startled. It was not their colour, which after he could not remember.

'And,' he repeated, losing his way, stumbling, 'and . . .'

'And give it to him, to keep his anger still in motion,' said Ellen Ternan.

'*Henry IV*,' said Dickens, intrigued.

'Hotspur,' smiled Ellen Ternan, for whom the Bard was as familiar as bedbugs.

Dickens stared at her for a moment. Later he found the memory of that moment irreducible to words.

'People forget Shakespeare was an actor first,' he said finally, when, frightened by those eyes, he had dropped his gaze back to the bird in her hands. 'And a writer only second. That is the secret of his genius. He had no sense of himself and existed only through his imitations of others.'

There, Dickens thought with an odd shock: I have given you the secret of myself. He stroked the bird, and he felt they both were paralysed with terror. He, who impressed countless thousands without effort, felt clumsy and awkward as he tried to make conversation with a young woman scarcely more than a child, whereas she felt emboldened.

'An eagle for an emperor,' said Ellen Ternan, continuing the game of quotation, 'a kestrel for a knave, and—' she paused; when Dickens lifted his eyes, for a second time she dared to look him directly in the face. 'A starling,' she smiled, 'a mimic for a writer.'

He turned away, somewhat flustered. Spotting a small pine box that was being used as a prop, he picked it up, as much to rid himself of the nervous energy that was suddenly surging through him as for any other reason. He took a handkerchief out of his pocket and formed a nest with it in the box, then placed the injured starling in its crinkled folds.

That evening, as he rode to dinner in a carriage with Catherine, he put his hand high up on his wife's skirted thigh. She turned and looked at him oddly, then pulled her leg away.

During what remained of the fortnight's rehearsals, Dickens spent an increasing amount of time in the proximity of Ellen Ternan. To be alone in her company was more difficult, but he contrived moments when others were absent and he unexpectedly present, when by seeming accident he bumped into her. At such times she found him delightful. She found him kind, always helpful, ever merry, and she never wondered why he was always finding her.

He thought her funny and lively; her forceful character, which so clearly irritated her mother, charmed him. Her straightforward judgements and strongly held opinions, and her interests in books and theatre and politics, seemed liberating after Catherine's professions of inescapable ignorance and stupidity and sullen silences. He saw that Ellen Ternan could also be childish, petulant and obstinate, that her feelings and ideas were sometimes shallow and foolish, but what irritated him in his wife delighted him in Ellen Ternan, and he excused that in which it was impossible for him to delight, for what did such trivialities matter? And not for a single moment did he think what his actions might mean—for, as long as he had no conscious intention, he was sure he could do no wrong.

Dickens' world seemed charged. It was the play, he told his friends as he had convinced himself—it was charity, it was the opportunity to help others combined with the joy of raising the production to a far more elevated level than he had ever anticipated. And his friends marvelled at his rediscovered energy, at the amount of time and attention he gave every aspect of the resurrected production, and particularly at the care he was lavishing on rehearsals. When at the end of the first week's rehearsal the starling vanished, presumably having gathered its strength and flown away, Dickens could not withhold the feeling that there was something liberating in the omen.

Yet he was enraged at the sheer lack of generosity his own wife showed towards the production.

'Why waste all this time on something that was working perfectly well before?' Catherine asked her husband one morning. She stood before him in his study with a vase of flowers. 'Look at these,' she said. 'Begonias and dahlias and all these beautiful annuals for your desk.' And when he didn't look up, she said, her tone suddenly cold, 'These Ternan women—if they are such good professionals, why do you need to be bothering rehearsing them so much?'

When Catherine stepped forward to place the vase down on the desk, her back, which had been bad since the birth of their second daughter, gave a sharp twinge. She stumbled and then dropped the vase, and flowers and water went spilling over a neat pile of writing.

Dickens leapt up and away from the puddling water. Frantically trying to rescue his pages, he muttered under his breath how she could not even keep house properly and it was no wonder that he was embarrassed to take her out into society.

But you haven't borne ten children, she wished to reply as she awkwardly got her balance back. You don't know what it does to you. You grow heavy, your memory wanders, your body leaks, your back burns. But she said none of it.

'I'm sorry, Charles,' she said, her voice shaking. 'I'm so sorry.'

As she mopped the table with her crinoline, she continued apologising. He shook a wet book that had been open on his desk. He asked her, was she that stupid? She wasn't. It was Carlyle's history of the French Revolution, dedicated to Dickens by the great historian himself. She knew he pored over it incessantly, once telling a visitor he had read it five hundred times. She stood there, not knowing what to do. She understood none of it. Surely he would be sick of the book by now.

Her mind seemed to be twisting into something so painful she had to hit her forehead with a fist in a vain attempt to reset the terrible clockwork of her life. She watched mute as her husband rang for a servant to come and clean up, then grabbed his coat and stormed out.

She realised she had never understood him. He was unstoppable, undeniable, he bent the world to his schemes and dreams as surely as he did his characters. And she knew that her part, henceforth, would be the fat and hopeless housekeeper, the hysteric, the invalid, the harridan and the virago.

Yet hadn't he, in every book and speech and utterance, said it was all about family and hearth and home? And hadn't she broken her body giving him children and trying to please him? Hadn't she loved him, and in his books wasn't such love always triumphant? She could not understand why in his home he had come to despise that same love as stupid.

And as she returned to gathering the strewn flowers, Catherine finally understood that she had been his invention as surely as any of the blurred pages on the desk, as much as any of those dull creatures he passed off as women in his books. He had made her stupid. He had made her that boring woman of his novels; she had become his heroine in her weakness and compliance and dullness.

Only now, having lived with her, he no longer liked that woman and wanted her gone. And she knew he would remake her with his wit, with his tongue, with his cruel names, and to the world she would be ridiculous and heartless. The world, she realised, was whatever Charles wanted. She had no defence.

She tried to rearrange the flowers. Larkspur, dahlias, cornflowers, sweet pea, begonias and baby's breath. She had gone in lockstep with it all—the ivy-clad cosy old house, the horde of children, the servants who had to be comical, him telling the world in his articles and speeches of their delightful Christmases, the endless merry times at the huge dinners for many. She had stuffed the mutton with oysters, made sure the cock-a-leekie was just as he liked it and the croquettes of chicken not lacking in imagination and the spiky pigeon feet poking perfectly like winter birch trees from the top of the pie. She had played along with all the games and the charades and leapfrogging. And yet, for everything good that had happened, so much more had for so long been ebbing out of her.

She remembered how, only the day before, he had

said she was turning the children against him, saying such wicked things, that she never cared for them properly, that she was mentally disordered. She was stupid, she knew, her back burnt, her heart leaked. Try as she might, none of the flowers came together in any pattern as the world swam in a cruel whirlpool around her.

The front door slammed and Katy came into the study to find her mother alone, both she and the vase of flowers she held in disarray. She looked half-mad; she was gasping, as though she were suffocating. Oblivious to her daughter, Catherine summoned from some void deep within a terrible sound, not a woman's voice, but some desolation far older. As though a thing infinitely precious had been stolen from her, she abruptly cried out—

'*It hurts!*'

And then said no more.

That night, Dickens came to bed late and lay for some time on his back. Neither touched. When she was almost asleep, she felt him slowly, almost absent-mindedly unlacing her nightgown. She reached out to him. She brought his face into her breasts. He smelt the lavender oil with which she perfumed herself every evening. She did not feel his tears. He was recalling Danton: *You do not make a revolution with rosewater.*

Away with a shriek and a roar and a rattle from the town they now fled, burrowing at first among the dwellings of men and making the streets hum, flashing out into meadows, mining in through the damp earth, booming on in darkness and heavy air, bursting out again into the sunny day so bright and wide. Fleeing through the hay, through the rock, through the woods, past objects almost in the grasp and ever flying from the traveller, Dickens felt a deceitful distance growing within him, while Ellen Ternan felt she was finally moving towards what life should be: joyous, exciting and so much fun.

On that train trip north in the month of August 1857, with *The Frozen Deep*'s large company and entourage taking several carriages, Dickens even had Mrs Ternan crying with laughter playing Conundrums, the answers for which he insisted on being passed window to window poised on umbrellas and walking sticks. When they were lost in the rushing wind he would run back and forth, pretending to tear out his hair in anguish, mimicking a lisping conductor by crying out, 'What a conundwum! My! My! What a wetched conundwum!'

And if such innocence were tinged with a flirtatious frisson, what of it? Ellen Ternan might enjoy his attentions as the tribute she was discovering men would pay to youthful beauty. But that was all. And Dickens, for his part, might play, possibly even tease, perhaps indulge in a certain kind of romance that permitted no sense of romantic attachment, and it would end, because his disciplined heart demanded no less. Destiny's darker edges were as Dickens was, dancing the sailor's hornpipe just as the train swerved around a great bend and tossed him into a corner: something simply to laugh at. What blow or fall could not be met and overcome with good humour? They were joyously alive and oblivious to everything, even as the world around them began to change by imperceptible degrees into something altogether different.

As the most famous Englishman of the age rolled around the floor of a train carriage, the eyes of those travelling with him were wet with tears of laughter. The train shrieked and cried louder and louder as it tore on resistless, until its way was strewn thickly with ashes and everything grew blackened. Around the train arose some strange charred forest from which humanity had simultaneously been exiled and was condemned henceforth to survive in.

Beyond the train windows, the filthy smoke writhed around battered roofs and broken windows and they could see into wretched rooms where want and fever hid themselves in many awful forms with death ever present, and Dickens turned away and tried not to think of what Wilkie had once said to him in an unguarded moment, that he lived as he acted, with a dead father in one pocket and a dead daughter in the other, unable to erase the image of either from his mind.

'Never ever this late,' Mrs Ternan was saying over and over, as she bustled Ellen and her two sisters into the smoke and noise of Manchester Railway Station two days later. 'Who knows whether they'll still be here?'

They strode through the crowd and, though Ellen's preparations for the outing had delayed them all and cost her a great deal of effort, to say nothing of her begging and pleading and more than a few moments of tears, she was now revelling in walking so purposefully through the carbon and sulphur haze, slightly sweet and somewhat damp, riding the trill excitement of clanging iron and sudden whistles past trembling platforms.

Though virtually none of what Ellen wore was hers, from the moment she walked down into the lobby of the Great Western Hotel that morning with her sisters and drew admiring glances, it felt as if the marble silk crinoline dress she had borrowed from her sister Fanny, with its beautiful sloping shoulders and elegant trim of lace ruche, had been made just for her, as though the long burgundy mantilla her mother had worn when she was younger and which now draped over her shoulders had always belonged to her.

She felt a perfect balance between this glorious costume and her life, her soul and the world. She was aware of the looks she was getting, but she had grown up on the stage and welcomed the attention. She smiled, as much with pleasure at her own appearance as with happiness, when she caught sight of a bearded face on the opposite platform suddenly bobbing up and smiling as their eyes caught—Mr Dickens! And at that moment, the noise grew intolerable and the platform began shaking as a locomotive rolled in, its coupling rod slowing, an oil-blackened engineer leaning out, his white eyes shining like lamplights as the great machine trundled between them.

As the train cut off the sight of the young woman, a

large, heavy man turned to Dickens and, leaning down into his ear, more yelled than whispered:

'In a word, the love of dress is the ruin of a vast number of young women.'

'Repression may well be the only lasting philosophy,' said Dickens. 'But, dear Mammoth, it is not the basis I propose to tell others to live their lives upon.' He was standing at the centre of a small party he had assembled for an outing to what was being billed as the greatest art exhibition in history, a show so large a building at Old Trafford had been erected especially for it, along with a new railway station for the visiting crowds.

'I beg for colour,' said Dickens, smiling and slightly bowing to the approaching Ternans. 'I crave colour in these cast-iron days.' He held out his hand and walked forward to the elegant ensemble. 'For a moment I thought it was the Empress Eugenie herself,' he said, taking hold of Ellen Ternan's hand, knowing full well—because she had told him—how she modelled her fashion on that of the young French monarch.

Perhaps it was the freedom of the wondrous steel hoops as opposed to the miles of petticoats his wife wore to keep her dresses puffed out, perhaps it was her youth, or perhaps, he wondered a little fancifully, it was her marvellous spirit, but she moved so freely and lightly, so nimbly and quickly, with her waist so fine. He recalled hearing how a woman had died wearing just such a skirt after she brushed against a candle and the dress went up like a hayrick, but now it was he who was burning.

Realising he was not charming but staring, Dickens dropped Ellen Ternan's hand, made a small leap like a startled bird, and hastened to divert attention from his momentary lapse.

'Mrs Ternan! What delights await us!' And then he spoke to Maria, he passed compliments to Fanny, and in the end a frustrated Ellen burst out—

'Mr Dickens! Do you or do you not like my pomegranate mantilla?'

'Red,' said Forster, unable to contain himself. 'And a dark red, at that, is not pomegranate.'

'I am told it is the traditional colour for brides in India,' said Ellen Ternan, wrapping a curl of her blonde hair around an index finger and not bothering even to look at Forster, but eyeing Dickens and smiling as she spoke. 'Its virtue could not be more widespread.'

As they made their way into the Manchester Art Treasures Exhibition, Dickens was reminded of some fabulous cross between the most modern railway station and the wonder of Ali Baba's cave. It was the spectacle of it all, the crowds, the human heat of the thing that excited Dickens far more than the endless old masters, the illustrious moderns, the sixteen thousand works of genius racked row above row, room after room.

Forster became dizzy viewing and was about to resort to the refreshment room for some boiled beef and bitter when they stopped by an old master's painting of Leda and the Swan, hung, as were all the salacious old masters, on the highest row.

'It is believed to be a copy of a lost Michelangelo original,' said Wilkie, passing to Ellen Ternan the opera glasses he had brought along to better admire the loftier works.

'I never really understood this myth,' said Mrs Ternan. 'A bad thing that somehow is seen to be good.'

A young man missing both legs and clad in rags trundled up beside them in a cut-down wooden barrel on wheels, which he paddled along with rudely bandaged hands. He reminded Dickens of a Russian samovar and interested him rather more than the paintings.

'Harmony and discord is what it means,' said Forster, who felt the need to offer commentary on everything. Wilkie raised his eyes and moved on to the next gallery. 'But mostly discord,' continued Forster. 'As a result of Zeus's crime, Leda conceived two eggs, and out of each egg were born two babies: one was Helen of Troy and I can't remember the others. Trojan war follows, destruction of a people. And so on. That's what it means.' And with that he disappeared to the refreshments room.

The samovar suddenly sneezed violently and Maria Ternan was caught up in the dreadful spray. Without waiting to apologise, he swung his barrel around and rolled away. Mrs Ternan and Maria and Fanny moved off to the other end of the room.

Through the jittery glass Ellen Ternan first saw two pairs of babies, each just hatched from an egg, and then her gaze rose above them to a subservient swan happy in the embrace of a serene and naked young woman. It wasn't as Forster had said at all, she thought. Everybody and everything in the painting—the babies, the swan, the world—all seemed to exist in awe of the naked woman. Ellen Ternan blushed, and the childlike colour it brought to her open face caught Dickens' eye as she passed the opera glasses to him.

'I could eat those babies,' said Ellen Ternan.

They were now by themselves. In the solitude that the odd tumult of a crowd offers, Dickens opera-glassed and, lost with distant thoughts, was momentarily unguarded. She could hear him sucking his tongue.

'She would be seven now,' he said.

'Who?' asked Ellen Ternan.

Dickens brought the glasses down and looked at her, embarrassed.

'I am sorry,' he said. 'Our daughter, Dora. When she was born she was so fresh you half expected to find eggshell on her crown.'

'I haven't met Dora,' said Ellen Ternan.

Dora was something Dickens didn't talk about, not even with Catherine. It wasn't reducible to risible anecdote or ridiculous dialogue. Against her death he seemed to be able to offer neither defence nor explanation. But that day he found himself telling the short story of her life brickfaced, with few words, ending with him leaving her sick that fateful day of his speech to the General Theatrical Fund.

'We have in our lives only a few moments,' said Dickens, but then he stopped. Words for him were songs, a performance. But he was not singing or performing now. 'A moment of joy and wonder with another. Some might say beauty or transcendence.' He swallowed. He had been talking about Dora, but now he realised it was about something else. 'Or all those things. Then you reach an age, Miss Ternan, and you realise that moment, or, if you are very lucky, a handful of those moments, was your life. That those moments are all, and that they are everything. And yet we persist in thinking that such moments will only have worth if we can make them go on forever. We should live for moments, yet we are so fraught with pursuing everything else, with the future, with the anchors that pull us down, so busy that we sometimes don't even see the moments for what they are. We leave a sick child in order to make a speech.'

He stopped talking, put the opera glasses to his eyes, then took them away. He looked not at Ellen Ternan, but straight ahead at the wall.

'The thing is,' he said, but he said no more.

It was then Ellen Ternan told him something no one had. It was as if she had heard something beyond his words. It felt like an absolution.

'You're not to blame,' said Ellen Ternan.

9

ON HEARING THE DOOR creak open—the vice-regal mansion's ramshackle nature meant it moved up and down and sideways, and, in consequence, everything was loose or jammed or, improbably, often somehow both—Sir John turned from the window, where he had been watching a storm front make its way up the Derwent. Lady Jane was looking at him with her eerie light-blue eyes, which he had once, if only for a short time, found so enchanting, but whose odd expression he came to realise he would never understand.

'You'll pay,' said Sir John.

'What do you—'

'What?' snapped Sir John, who now remembered what he had been trying to recall for the previous several minutes. 'What Montague said to me, that's what. That I'd pay.' Once Sir John had prided himself that he forgot nothing. Now he had trouble recalling even a small thing said a few moments before. More strangely, large things once simple and obvious were becoming ever more diffuse and vaporous. And just as reports and memoranda more and more frequently blurred as he stared intently at them, he had the disconcerting impression that so too was his wife now blurring and dissolving into a stranger.

'When did Montague say such a thing?' he could hear her asking.

'When I refused his nephew a land grant,' said Sir John. 'That's when. And after Pedder's brother-in-law was not awarded the wharf contract, he said something similar.'

'But that was years ago—' Lady Jane began, but Sir John was waving a hand back and forth in a gesture of futility.

'And now he and our enemies have triumphed,' he said. 'It is beyond imagining.'

Outside, a storm of terrible force finally broke. Several boats were sunk in the chaos, houses unroofed, trees blown over, drays and carts tossed about as if children's toys. A fine bay stallion owned by Mr Lord was impaled when a spar was tossed like a toothpick from an adjacent sawpit into the poor beast's belly. And inside Sir John's head, the dark cloud of a growing melancholy broke now into a storm just as ferocious, as hopes, desires and memories were thrown hither and thither, smashing his sense of himself as a good man and a noble leader. As much as to battle an odd vertigo that had suddenly enveloped him as to explain himself, Sir John picked up some official papers and brandished them in front of Lady Jane.

'It has not been as it should,' he said, and his voice was for a moment—but only a moment—a snarl. 'Here,' he said, rustling the papers. Then he dropped them as though they were burning his fingers. 'Orders arrived from the Colonial Office this morning. Signed by the Secretary himself.' His body was shaking, almost wobbling with rage. 'I am to be recalled.'

And having said this, Sir John felt suddenly spent. Lady Jane shot him a look he recognised as being at once utter shock and pure contempt. And how, he wondered, am I to blame for a humiliation as public as this? He recalled their triumphant reception on first arriving in Hobart, the accolades, the extraordinary joy as if he were liberating the people from a tyrant. And yet deep within his soul he sensed his crime was somehow linked to his failure to offer the reassurance of a new tyranny.

'Why?' asked Lady Jane, her voice implacable iron.

It was bewildering, thought Sir John. What was it Crozier had said in his cups? *You set out to discover a new land because you sense you have always been lost.*

'Because . . . it seems they have persuaded the Colonial Secretary I am incompetent and corrupt and—'

'But in truth?'

'In truth? Perhaps because I wasn't corrupt. But I've been a fool.'

'Until you took this wretched commission in this godforsaken island,' said Lady Jane suddenly, and uncharacteristically furious, 'we had no enemies. We were sought as ornaments to power, never disposed of as its necessary sacrifice.'

It was true he had not sought the commission, that all this was his wife's work—but then, his entire life since meeting her had been her work. She had relieved him from his most secret vice, his own immeasurable lack of ambition. Was he to blame for that? For submitting to her so completely? He had once overheard Montague say he was a 'weak character'. And was not this the unspoken heart of the Colonial Secretary's accompanying letter, in which he wrote of '*the inappropriate weight given to others*'?

This confused Sir John more than anything else. Was it weakness to be at ease with what life brought—be it suffering and starvation in the polar ice, or pleasing another human being by doing as she wished—or was it wisdom?

'Trust to it,' Montague had said when they first arrived, gesturing with a thin arm in the direction of the dilapidated capital and, beyond it, the ceaseless vegetation walling in the city, the endless nameless mountains, the mapless rivers.

But trust to what? A weird land predating time, with its vulgar rainbow colours, its vile, huge forests and bizarre animals that seemed to have been lost since Adam's exile?

Or had Montague meant the people—the brutes that served him, waited on him, acted as clerks and flagellators and cooks and barbers and just about everything else? They were all convicts, a grotesque parody, a hideous pantomime, a revolting insult to memory; and that, in Sir John's eyes, made them only more ridiculous in their imitation of all things England. He could see they were becoming something else, though, as savage as the savages, and out in the backblocks, it was said, they were regressing to a similar way of life, dressing in kangaroo skins, living in clans, sleeping in bark huts, working only to kill the native animals on which they subsisted. Oh, he had trusted to it all right, Sir John thought bitterly, trusted too much and for too long, and now he was paying the price.

As Lady Jane walked to the door, she halted, seemed to ponder something, then turned.

'The black girl,' she said.

Sir John felt such a phrase did not augur well. Lady Jane spoke of 'Mathinna' when she was happy with her, which was rarely, and 'the black girl' when she wasn't, which these days was frequently.

'I see even you've given up on her.'

Sir John seemed to be thinking.

'Those strange vapours that seized her on the *Erebus* last year,' Lady Jane went on. 'It seems they affected her badly.'

Sir John waited.

'It is a kind of hysteria she contracted,' she said. 'Do you not think so?'

Sir John was unsure.

'Rather than getting better quickly, as one might have expected with a white child,' said Lady Jane, 'she has grown worse.'

As the weeks had become months, Sir John knew, Mathinna had learnt to avoid being seen, and if seen, how to amuse without offence. She had become more like a pet than a child in the house.

'Listless,' said Lady Jane.

He knew that Mathinna no longer pushed herself forward, grabbed legs or hid behind dresses. That what remained of her routines and schedules had crumbled under the weight of her sullen refusal to engage with anything she was shown or taught. That she was terrified of him.

'And wild,' said Lady Jane. 'An animal that attacks the servants. Hitting and screaming and scratching. She even bit one of the serving maids, Mrs Wick, and when compelled to resume her daily schedule, she was slovenly and withdrawn. It is as though the sickness has affected her very soul.'

Then for the first time both the Franklins understood something in Mathinna's behaviour as the most public defeat of their time in Van Diemen's Land. For the black child would not become white.

'She is exasperation,' said Lady Jane.

'It is beyond explanation,' replied Sir John.

'God knows how she will fare in London,' said Lady Jane. And with that, she turned again and left the room.

Sir John returned to the window and the pewter haze of rain. Down on the street, a beggar had taken off his ragged coat and was holding it over the head of an old crone as they hurried away. How at that moment Sir John envied the beggar his selflessness, his very life! And in this endless world that teemed with so much life, so much love, with so many things, he realised he was alone.

A manservant appeared with coffee.

'Later.'

There was about the island, his position, his own faded ambitions, the utterly unjustified reputation he carried with him as an ever-heavier burden, something intolerable and entirely absurd. It was baffling, as he increasingly found most human things to be. Sir John had at his disposal one regiment of some six hundred soldiers, half of whom were drunks and all of whom were dissatisfied. Yet these few unreliable men kept some tens of thousands of convicts subjugated—or, rather, the tens of thousands of convicts subjugated themselves. Why, it was as miraculous and ridiculous as anything in the world! But in their meek complicity he saw his own nature amplified—after all, he had passed most of his life imprisoned in the desires and dreams of others.

An aide-de-camp appeared to remind him of—

'Later.'

As Sir John sat in his dimming study, slumped on a sagging chaise, he resented the Van Diemonians in general and just about everyone he knew in particular: his wife, Montague, Mathinna—especially Mathinna. He despised and loathed them all and simply wanted to be gone from them, far away. How he longed to flee back to the comforting old dream of being with a small band of men in the ice, where he was free of such things. He sat there a long time, alone, silent. As the light ebbed, as the dark advanced, it slowly became clear to him who was responsible.

'The savage,' he hissed.

Of course, he thought. One always had enemies, that was clear; he should have given them land and contracts, and more besides. That too was clear. But in this instance they had been armed.

And by whom? The savage had caused his downfall. How had he not seen it? The monster had seen an opportunity to destroy him and seized it, signalling with her behaviour—at first so obviously intoxicating him with some magic, and then disparaging him—yes, it was she whose actions had fed the rumours, armed his enemies, created the scandal that had led to this pretty pass. Montague may have fired the gun, but Sir John could now see it was Mathinna's witchery that had primed his shot.

Yet this terrible thought left Sir John oddly cold and quiet. Outside, the storm subsided to a fitful drizzle. All that remained was the sound of a pod of spouting whales in the vast river beyond, followed by the distant cries of the whaling boats and the harpooners beginning the slaughter.

Five years hence, Sir John would recall this moment as one of an infinite peace. As he lay in Crozier's cabin on the ice-bound *Erebus*, he heard the slow cracking and terrifying splintering of timbers under impossible pressure. The ship was pitched wildly to its side by the ice, his cot jammed level between the wall and floor, with wood and ice and wind groaning and shrieking their fatal destiny ceaselessly. An intolerable mist full of the moist black stench of gangrene spread from beyond his cabin into the midships.

Inside, on the same cot on which Mathinna once lay before him in a pretty red dress, the great polar explorer rolled back the covers and his bandages with a mixture of horror and fascination, to investigate by the greasy whale-oil light the stinking stump that had once been him.

In his final agony, Sir John's thoughts were only of catching birds with a small dark girl who still laughed at him, and his head momentarily filled with the improbable smell of a world that he now recalled as Eden after rain. His mind was a jumble of so many good things, cockatoos and whales and children, when suddenly he saw the cabin he was being tortured within, the cot he was dying in, a rumpled red dress, a whimpering wallaby face. There came to him a sense of his own horror. Cold was crossing his skin, invading his being, fine shards of ice were already webbing his lungs.

'South by west,' he began quickly chanting, as if it might redeem him, as though it were a lodestone that might yet point the way to an escape. 'South-southwest, southwest by—' But then there erupted from him a sudden sound of infinite dread that rose and fell in the eerie dark beyond, then was lost forever. By the time Crozier rushed into his cabin, camphor-soaked handkerchief firmly clasped over his own wasted face, the greatest explorer of his age was already dead.

That evening, Sir John was relieved that they had guests for dinner, including Edward Kerr, an agent of the Van

Diemen's Land Company, a party of London investors that owned the northwestern quarter of the island. Kerr had arrived on a hard-ridden roan horse, and everything about him suggested a muscularity of character and purpose that Sir John, ill-assembled and worse-starred, admired. The Governor made no mention of his own fate; that, he decided, could wait for official proclamation in the *Gazette*. Though Mathinna's gradual abandonment of decorum and her slovenly dress meant she no longer attended formal dinners, one of the guests had seen her hanging upside down in a tree near the entry circle.

'I do believe,' said Lady Jane tersely, when mention was made of this, 'that some effort to save them from extinction must be made, and that it is for us to offer an example.'

'Why, Lady Jane, you are aware,' said another voice, 'that some of the blacks' most brutal leaders were those we raised as Christian children. Just look at Black Tom who went over to the blacks and became a perfect brute.' It was the solicitor-general, a man whose name Sir John constantly muddled with an old friend's, one further defect in the eyes of his growing number of enemies. 'I was only reluctantly drawn into the debate, but I argued to your husband's predecessor, Governor Arthur, that the government had a legal duty to protect its convicts, who were vulnerable to attack working out in the hinterlands.'

'And what did you advise, Mr Tulle?' asked Lady Jane.

'That if you cannot do so without extermination, then, I said, exterminate. There was no safety for the white man but through the destruction of his black opponent. We put a bounty on their heads for several years. Good money. Five pounds a head.'

'My whole and sole object in those heroic years was to kill them,' said Kerr over the wombat consommé, in a refreshingly frank and, Sir John felt, welcome manner. At this point Lady Jane rose, said she had had a long day, and with a smile excused herself. Kerr then showed himself to be that most necessary of middle-aged men for a frozen social event: the raconteur oblivious to the sentiments of others. After rising to farewell Lady Jane and rather dashingly kissing her hand, he was again seated and holding forth with his reflections.

'And this,' continued Kerr, pointing his soup spoon, as presumably he once pointed a pistol, 'because my full conviction was and is that the laws of nature and of God and of this country all conspired to render it my duty.'

His gentle voice, his calm, almost reserved manner, his boyish, wavy blond hair, his near absolute absorption in his own experience—all somehow combined with the shocking violence of his story to give his words a mesmerising charm.

'As to my having three of their heads on the ridge of my hut, I shall only say that I think it had the effect of deterring some of their comrades, of making the deaths of their companions live in their recollections, and so extended the advantage the example made of them.'

Franklin realised Kerr was an extraordinary man. He could not have known it without living for so long as he had on the island, but now everything was clear to him in a way it never had been before. There was an honesty about Kerr that was bracing, even thrilling—he knew it, he exuded and exhaled a terrifying self-belief—what man with three heads staked on top of his home does not?

And in his candour, thought Franklin, was some terrible truth that was compelling, some strange combination of desire and freedom, some acceptance not of peace but of the violence of which Sir John increasingly feared he himself was inexorably composed, the violence that he had begun to believe was the true motor of the world, the violence he sensed but could not admit to himself was at the heart of what had passed between him and Mathinna. It was not the violence that was wrong, thought Sir John, it was the lack of courage in not carrying it through to its logical end, as Kerr so forthrightly did. Sir John envied Kerr's serenity in accepting his own wretched destiny; he wanted such serenity, such certainty. He turned away from this strange hero of the Black War and pondered his own future where what Crozier had called 'that crystal desert of oblivion' beckoned.

'We are the emissaries of God, science, justice,' continued Kerr. 'We know pity and the Devil knows what else. But nothing beats three staked heads. What was it that young naturalist Darwin said when he visited here a few years past and sat in this very dining room? "Van Diemen's Land enjoys the great advantage of being free from a native population." You think such freedom easily won? Perhaps you think it can happen without several staked heads.'

Kerr smiled. His mica eyes betrayed nothing yet told everything: he had the chilling certainty of a man unafraid of the horror he has discovered in himself.

Sir John sensed in Kerr's profound judgements something that went beyond good and evil. But the Christian pity and scientific curiosity of him and his wife, which had led them to adopt Mathinna—would not such virtues be rewarded?

'I think not,' said Kerr, and it was as if that extraordinary man had read Sir John's very thoughts.

Sir John smiled. There was a thing pitiless and intolerable that he felt the island brought out in men; the wild lands, the seas, all seemed to draw a man's soul to something beyond its own normal boundaries, perhaps even to demand it. And tonight this thought pleased him. Sir John could feel the attraction, the immense satisfaction of being a soul that answered to no creed, that knew no rules, the power of being a small god that he had first sensed in Robinson, that he had since seen in the large free settlers with their feudal farms, the sealers with their harems of black women.

'People come here to get on, you see,' said Kerr.

Sir John did see, and it was as if he were seeing it all for the first time, but it was too late. The gods were created by just such brigands and rapists in their own image, to serve them and their needs.

'They don't want to take in the sublime wilds and delude themselves they can enlighten those who have lived in the darkness of the woods too long,' Kerr went on, now drumming a martial beat on the table with his soup spoon. 'You understand, of course.'

Sir John did understand. And he, who had been determined about little in his life, was now determined Lady Jane would too.

Subsequently, Sir John's departure was so dignified that it won him the respect he had never known as Governor. He showed no sign of anger, nor shame, nor rage, at what all now said were so clearly the wicked manipulations of the Arthur faction. It was almost as if he welcomed his fate, and he seemed to demonstrate in his going so much that had been absent in his administration.

It was noted with approval how Sir John was finally decisive with his wife on the matter of the black child, who, he now said, would not be taken with them to England. He declared medical opinion against it: experience showed savages' bodies were constitutionally incapable of surviving a robust climate; it was as proven and undeniable as were the advantages she had enjoyed which would ensure her future was bright indeed. He did not involve his wife in the matter of the memorandum ordering that the child be taken away to St John's Orphanage. He would not hear her protests, but observed that it was as fine an institution as had ever been erected, and that the child would there be able to finish her education to the satisfaction of all. He would not enter into an argument with Lady Jane about the experiment being not yet ended.

'It was unscientific yearnings from the beginning,' Sir John said, and though the word they both knew he intended was *mad*, there was about his statement the tone of undeniable conviction. When Lady Jane said that she must prepare the child, and went to assure her that her destiny was still promising, it was already too late. They had taken Mathinna the morning before, without warning or explanation, but with the precaution of giving her a special breakfast of toasted cheese. Whether this was to calm the fear she might have or to assuage the guilt he possessed, he was unsure: he simply felt it an act born of necessity, rather than nostalgia.

Sir John walked over to the large log fire to warm himself as his aide-de-camp now told him of the morning's petitioners, nodding agreement here, shaking his head there, while happily dreaming all the time of the ice to which he knew he could now return. The polar regions existed beyond politics and progress; doubt visited every day, but had little choice but to leave quickly. The emptiness invited simple decisions, and required that these be honoured with inordinate courage; for the decisions were momentous but not complex, and in spite of all the talk of discovery, of survival, it was a world of lost children whose failures were celebrated as the triumphs of men.

And at the pleasant thought of absconding from adulthood, of returning to an implacable solitude as if to the womb, to an inevitable oblivion that by the strangest alchemy of a nation's dreaming would inexorably become celebrity and history, he smiled again and called for his glass once more to be filled, all the while trying to halt his hand from trembling.

Winter was upon the island, the snow low on the mountain, and while a man dreamt of returning to being a child, there was huddled in the back of a jolting dray a shivering girl leaving the tattered remnants of her childhood behind forever. She was clutching a possum-skin rug around her to keep at bay the driving sleet, to deny an ever-encroaching solitude that felt increasingly like death. She knew only what little she had been told: so that her experience of other children might be broadened, she was being boarded for a few days at a nearby school, and was to take nothing with her, neither possessions nor pets. It was, the child realised, odd, but little about her life wasn't.

Mathinna lay down, curled into the rug, closed her eyes and let her frail shell of a body ride the bumps and jolts. She told herself she was warm and safe and, consoled by such necessary untruths and with the comforting fullness of toasted cheese in her belly to further the illusion, she somehow fell asleep and dreamt of running through wallaby grass.

When she awoke, the horse was straining its traces, pulling the cart up a steep, muddy road towards a lonely building that burst out of the dark earth like the head of a broad arrow. The oppressive solitude of St John's Orphanage seemed heightened by the dark forests and snow-mantled mountain that wrapped around it. At its centre was a sandstone church with a tall steeple, on either side of which the children's dormitories—boys on the right, girls on the left—fell away like broken wings.

That most children there weren't orphans, but illegitimate or unlucky with careless parents, was hardly the point. Though St John's was intended to be for children without virtue, in practice it was for those without defence, children who had annoyed the authorities by running through the streets of Hobart Town unattended, by playing, in imitation of their adult betters, games of flogging and hanging and bushranging. They were now rounded up and locked away at St John's.

Every day began with church, and the church stalls had been built to stop moral pollution of any kind. The boys could not see the girls, and the convicts and all the massed undesirables were kept out of sight of the pious free settlers from the nearby enclave of the newly rich, which was called, appropriately and dismally, New Town. While the fireplaces were arranged around the free settlers' pews, those designated orphans were denied even the possibility of movement to keep warm. They offered up prayers for the wicked and the fallen, the lost and broken, the sick and the invalid, the poor fatherless and miserable motherless children, and afterwards they went back to cough and freeze and be beaten once more.

On the day Mathinna arrived, the church service had been held over an hour late because the typhoid had claimed another child overnight, bringing the total who had died in the previous month to five. There was a listlessness about the whole place that subdued even the sharp scent of imminent violence normally permeating the building. Mathinna was told nothing about what was happening to her, nor what place it was through which she now walked with a lack of concern that only someone who did not realise this was her destiny could manifest. She was led down a dark corridor that tunnelled through the building and opened out onto a veranda at the back, and there told only to wait.

She looked out over a squalid yard. Though muddy that winter's day, it still drew the children as a place where one could, if not get warm, then at least gaze on the distant heat of an even more distant sun. Warmth was, for the children, an idea—the one philosophy they were introduced to at St John's—and from an unshadowed corner, two skiving boys, seeking to acquaint themselves better with it, turned to stare at the new arrival.

As Mathinna stood there, possum-skin rug wrapped around her, feeling sleepy and queasy from the cart ride, she noticed a sulphur-crested cockatoo alight on a rusting whaling try-pot set below a dripping gutter. Mathinna's eyes sharpened. The bird was clearly an escaped pet, for it jumped from foot to foot while alternately crying out 'Love youse!' and 'Fug youse!' It was a beautiful large parrot, its coat fine, its bearing splendid.

Mathinna smiled, as if at the sight of a friend. She stepped forward, her hand proffered as a perch, and the bird cocked its head and turned a glistening ebony eye at her, then threw up its sulphur crest in greeting. It had taken two hops towards her when it was felled by a rock. Mathinna looked up and saw a smiling boy proudly waving a slingshot, then back at the parrot convulsing in the mud. She leant down and with a single quick movement wrung its neck, then turned away, and abruptly doubling up, vomited cheese and toast into the try-pot.

Some time later she was fetched by an old man with a gammy leg, who, hobbling and cursing as they went, took her up flights of bare pine stairs to a storeroom stacked with clothing. Here she showed the first signs of resistance after Mrs Trench, a woman of great girth and gasping speech, attempted to take off Mathinna's green seashell necklace and red dress, her best clothes that she had worn for the occasion. Mathinna bit Mrs Trench's hand so hard it bled. The Warden was summoned but was a good hour arriving, having been overseeing the burning of the forest behind St John's, from which he knew the foul, fatal typhoid miasma to be emanating.

Angry at his important work being interrupted, the Warden, a man of later years with the build and pocked face of an anvil, thrashed the child with a tea-tree stick for insolence, and, when the child would offer neither explanation nor apology for her animal behaviour, thrashed her a second time for dumb insolence. After, she was taken to a room kept specially for such malevolent offenders and locked there for the rest of the day and the night. Without bed, hammock or palliasse, its sole furnishing was an unfired chamber pot, cracked such that it leaked over the already putrid floor on which she slept.

The following morning, Mrs Trench, aided by two wardsmen who each took an arm, dragged Mathinna to the washroom. There, with the wardsmen holding her down as she bucked and thrashed, Mrs Trench stripped the child, shoved her around a little in the name of looking for lice, and threw a bucket of cold water over her. Though Mathinna lost the fight, her struggle was recognised when Mrs Trench tossed her seashell necklace and red dress back at her, saying that as long as she wore something on top, she could keep them. Her head was then shaved of its dense black curls, and she was dressed in a stained blue gown and calico pinafore, both large enough to sit over her red dress and several more.

Because Mathinna was, in her way, a person of note, she was solemnly presented by the Warden with something few children received, a pair of wooden clogs, which had belonged to a boy who had died of fever during the night. Her only response was to throw them back at the Warden. After being thrashed again, she was taken barefoot to the punishment room for a second day and night with the cracked chamber pot.

Despite the Warden spending the rest of the day burning the forest behind the orphanage, despite the air by the afternoon being choked with smoke rather than the peaty aroma of forest, two more children were carried away with typhoid that evening. It was clear to all the staff, who heard it from Mrs Trench, and to all the children, who heard it from the staff—who knew it for a fact—that the blacks had 'powers'. Even more pervasive than the acrid taste of ash was the dread that now settled over the orphanage. Everyone knew that the sulking black child was exercising her vengeance.

The only conclusions to be drawn from the Warden's wise compromise the following day, when he thrashed Mathinna for a fourth time but then let the child witch doctor sleep in the dormitory with the other girls, were that the black girl was indeed an emissary of the Devil and that the Warden had won them all a reprieve from death. For the fatal contagion ended, and it was clear that while no amount of burnt forest had halted the plague, this one providential act had.

In the dormitory, the rich scent of ammonia rising from the damp hammocks of the bed-wetters, whose inexplicable sin defied all beatings, mingled that moonlit night with the swarms of strange insects that the island seemed to breed in biblical proportions—flying ants, moths the size of small birds, mosquitoes. The black girl's Satanic reputation was enhanced when she, who refused to eat of a day, of a night caught the moths with lightning strikes of her hand and gobbled them up.

In spite of Sir John telling Lady Jane he had been advised that visits of any type would only further distress the child and not help ease her into her new life, Lady Jane went to the orphanage three days later to retrieve Mathinna. She was motivated partly by wounded pride, by a measure— real but not large—of appropriate concern, and by a desire to remind her husband that such an action, taken without consultation, was unacceptable.

But there was something else; something buried so deep within Lady Jane that it took the form of a physical pain she did not dare seek words for. She was not an hysteric. She refused to open herself up to such morbid sensations as she had seen women of feeble character do, embracing the maladies of their own mind. But still it came on her in waves, leaving her short of breath and disoriented, as the Warden led her through the Orphanage's many rooms in accordance with the Governor's earlier instructions. For Sir John had lived too long with his wife's will to believe he would be obeyed, and so, as a seasoned naval officer, he had prepared a wily line of second defence.

The children slunk away from Lady Jane like animals, one part fearful and two parts desperate for food and life; the only sleek and content being she saw in this grove of misery was a large ginger tomcat, fat on the rats that even at this hour sported along the shadowed kickboards. Lady Jane tried to talk to one boy, but he seemed indifferent to her or anybody or anything, as though he had withdrawn from life. She asked other children: did they get enough to eat? was all well here?

But they seemed not to hear, far less comprehend. Their faces were subdued and empty, their skin chapped and often scabby, their expressions expressionless. Lady Jane noticed an eerie absence of whispering or pulling hair or giggling. The children seemed too exhausted to do much more than cough and hack and scratch, beset with everything from consumption to dysentery to chilblains, the tormented wounds of which scabbed their arms with bloodied buttercups.

Though the orphanage was but a few years old, there was a stench about it. Lady Jane could identify one scent as that of decay, but beyond it, over it, was another odour she could not name, that she would later describe in her diary only in the vaguest terms: the place smelt, she wrote, '*of something wrong*'. It was a smell trapped in the putrid canvas hammocks she now walked past in the stinking dormitory, their umber weave mottled with large florettes of urine and blood, it was embedded in the ammoniacal rough floor boards, it was embodied in a small mound of angry red and yellow flesh that lay in a rude cot in a corner, wrapped in lint and greased like a cold roast potato.

'House fire,' said the Warden in a low whisper. 'Mother burnt to death. Only girl saved.'

Apart from an occasional low, long whimper, the child gave no sign of pain or interest. Instead she merely stared at the ceiling with intensely vivid blue eyes that looked as if they had been mistakenly buried in charred pork, as if they were wondering why it was taking so long to be interred in one of the toy-sized coffins that waited, white-painted, racked and ready, in the cellar storeroom where Lady Jane was next taken.

'Marvellously and completely self-contained, we are,' said the Warden as he raised the lantern around his macabre store. 'Our boys make these themselves.'

Leaving the coffin room, Lady Jane asked to be excused

the rest of the tour, and so instead they went to the second-storey dining room, in which the officials of the institution took their meals and from where it was possible to look out on a rear courtyard where the children passed their idle time. Through the whirling glass she looked down on that muddy square.

Lady Jane swallowed.

Were it not for Mathinna's colour, she would not have recognised the already scabby, shaven-headed child in a drab cassock who sat alone and unmoving in the dirt below. When hit in the face by some mud hurled at her by another child, Mathinna bared her teeth and appeared to hiss, which, oddly, seemed to put an end to the attack.

Lady Jane had come to take her home. She did not care what her fool husband thought or did, or what the wretches that passed for colonial society might say. She had intended simply stating her desire and leaving immediately with Mathinna. But something stopped her from saying what she wished, from doing what she desired. Instead she said she hoped Mathinna was eating properly.

'Eating?' said the Warden, who had come to stand at the window with Lady Jane. 'Eats nothing. Except insects.'

There was a long silence. Even words seemed unnecessary luxuries at St John's.

'My dear Warden,' Lady Jane began, then halted and shook her head. She just wanted to leave.

The Warden leant in closer. 'Yes, Lady Jane?'

'Mr—how do I say this? The child never ate insects all the years she was with me.'

'She has reverted to type,' said Mrs Trench, who now joined them.

'Did she,' asked the Warden, 'hide her true nature from you? All those years? Is what we see below the truth of these people?'

They stared for a few moments without speaking at the mud-spattered, bedraggled girl. Lady Jane's vision began blurring, and she turned to face the Warden.

'She struck me as . . .' said Lady Jane, but some certainty, some conviction, was missing from her voice, from the words spilling from her mouth. She brushed her eyes with a kid-gloved finger. 'At least, initially, that is, she—she appeared intelligent, seemed—'

'Intelligent?' said the Warden, as though it were a matter to ponder. He seemed deeply understanding, and his understanding was somehow terrifying and impossible for Lady Jane. He smelt of smoke and sounded like clanging iron. 'No,' said the Warden finally. 'Never that.'

'Rat cunning, more like it,' said Mrs Trench.

'Animal instinct,' said the Warden, 'highly honed. As Mrs Trench—much experienced with the savages—has alluded to. Do we commit Rousseau's fallacy? Thinking rat cunning equates with humanity or civilisation? No. Why? Because when rewarded, the child pretended to one thing. But here we see that they are capable of the grossest deceit. Precisely *because* progress is impossible, they regress quickly.' He looked Lady Jane in the eyes and his thin lips slowly formed a pained smile of knowing compassion. 'Is this painful for you to hear? I know, Ma'am. How can it not be? But to us here at St John's Orphanage, they are all God's children. Wherever they come from, Ham or Abraham, it matters not.'

The Warden believed in God's love and pity. A terrible love. A most terrifying pity. And against all that belief and all that love and all that pity, against all the questions already answered, even a spirit as indomitable as Lady Jane's faltered.

She swung back to the swirling glass and the sight of Mathinna beyond, so buffeted by waves of memory and emotion she thought she might sink beneath them. How she longed again to hear the tinkling of the bell as the child made her way around the house. For arms wrapping around her legs and waist, grabbing and holding her. Why had she pushed the child away when she had secretly longed to be so grabbed and held?

And then she could no longer hold down that deep buried feeling. She could no longer deny the memory of her three miscarriages. She could not forget her grief, and then the cruel awakening to her barren body, her loneliness, her inescapable sense of shame as a woman, her desperate desire for a child, her pride that rescued her and then crushed her and made her move relentlessly and constantly, desperately seeking to raise herself and her husband forever after, as though they might somehow escape the gravity of her grief.

Until that day on Flinders Island when she had seen Mathinna dance in a white kangaroo skin, Lady Jane had deluded herself that it was science, reason, Christianity;

that the ruse of a noble experiment might somehow bring her the mystery that other women took for granted, but she never admitted what it really was that she longed to know: the love of a mother for a child.

She wished to rush down to the filthy courtyard, grab Mathinna and steal the frightened child away from all this love and pity, this universal understanding that it was necessary that she suffer so. She wished to wash and soothe her, to whisper that it was all right, over and over, that she was safe now, to kiss the soft shells of her ears, hold her close, feed her warm soup and bread. She wished to be the mother she had tried so hard never to appear, to put her nose in Mathinna's wild hair and comfort and protect her, and revel in her difference and not seek to destroy it, because in that moment she knew that the destruction of that difference could only lead, in the end, to the terrible courtyard below, and the white coffins below that.

Then this thought was replaced by a different voice that whispered how all these things were regrettable but unavoidable, that somehow the stinking hammocks and rats and cold mud and burnt children were for a necessary purpose. It made no sense. But finally her head succeeded in steadying her reckless heart. And Lady Jane recognised the truth of what she was being told: that her great experiment was the most ignominious failure, and that she must not suffer the further humiliation of taking Mathinna home to England. At that moment, everything in that room, in St John's, smelt to her of wet stone.

She turned away from the window and the sight of that filthy, bedraggled figure. She took a deep breath. None could ever underestimate her courage.

'What you say accords with common sense,' she said slowly, stumbling over the words as though it were a confession extracted by some terrible means. 'I can see that she is simply reverting to her animal nature.'

'It is what we have worked with before,' said the Warden gently. 'There are places for all in our colony's kitchens and sculleries, Ma'am. But you cannot raise gazelles from rats.'

Lady Jane could see that whatever magic Mathinna had possessed as a small girl on Flinders Island had now vanished. Now she was no longer pretty but dirty and unattractive, no longer delightful and happy but spiteful and miserable. In truth, thought Lady Jane, she has under my care only gone backwards, and can only degenerate further. The dance had left the dancer.

Watching Lady Jane's carriage return, seeing her enter Government House alone, Sir John hoped he would be seen as callous by more than just his wife. It would help—if only in a small way—restore his standing with the colonists, and with that, he might find some small measure of pride restored. He despised himself for it and despised humanity for it. He recognised it as a conclusive argument for his return to something for which he was in every other respect congenitally unsuited—by weight, by age, by character—the white world of polar exploration. It was the only emptiness he knew greater than himself.

———

The day after they sailed from Van Diemen's Land, when there was enough sea between them and the child, in an act that was composed equally of contrition and cunning, Sir John made a gift to his wife of a painting of Mathinna done by the convict Bock shortly before the fateful ball.

She was wearing her favourite red dress, and the picture was marred only by one detail: her bare feet. For Mathinna had, typically, kicked off her court shoes for the sitting and Bock had painted her barefooted. Because it was a watercolour, he did not feel he could paint shoes over the feet, and when, on Lady Jane's instructions, Bock painted a copy with shoes, it had somehow lost the delightful spontaneity of the original. And so the paintings had been rolled up and stored away and forgotten, until Sir John had the original searched out and framed.

'It really is a fine likeness of the child when she was at her most admirable,' he said as the wrapping paper fell to the floor. 'Predating her rather sorry decline.'

Lady Jane wanted to scream.

With a piece of shaped timber, the framer had achieved more in a moment than she had with her previously invincible will over the last five years. His oval frame neatly cut Mathinna off at her ankles and finally covered her bare feet.

Lady Jane stepped out of the dimness of their cabin into the intense daylight of the quarterdeck. There was a beautiful freshness about the sun, the ship, the wind, the sea. It was as though the world had been born anew. The freshly washed decks steamed; the light broke the sea into a million diamonds.

She turned and strode to the stern. With an uncharacteristically violent motion, she threw the painting in the wake of the ship. It dipped and rode the air as it fell. For a moment it seemed as if it might fly. Then it smacked into the sea, tearing on impact. It quickly drifted away, face down. When she turned, Sir John was standing behind her, black streaks across his forehead as the wind blew his long greased hairs into writhing question marks.

It was 1844. The last pair of great auks in the world had just been killed, Friedrich Nietzsche born, and Samuel Morse sent the first electrical communication in history. It was a telegram that read: *What hath God wrought*.

'I loved her,' said Lady Jane.

IO

DICKENS STOOD ON THE STAGE which would soon transport him to the Arctic, and looked around that marvellous magic theatre. The Manchester Free Trade Hall was as remarkable as anything else in that great shock-city, which, with its huge factories, foundries and mills, its slums, its misery and its riches, was the wonder of the modern world. The theatre had every modern appliance and device. Far above him, a gasman sat on the trapeze fly at his table, operating the best set of gas borderlights and footlights Dickens had seen, while to his left on a perch was the very latest theatrical innovation, a limelight.

Two men stood by that large box of burning lime, their job to keep its fire burning with a giant pair of bellows, prevent the temperamental machine from exploding, while all the time moving its dazzling cone of brilliant white light hither and thither around the stage. Dickens had only heard of this amazing contrivance, and now here he was, about to play within its extraordinary glow.

He stood a desk johnny at centre stage, had the limelight lit and focused on the man's face. The limelight's power was extraordinary. It washed colour out. It accentuated wrinkles, jaws, lips. It was clear to Dickens that his make-up would need to be stronger, more pronounced, to take full advantage. He went to the back of the stalls and had the johnny drop and raise his head, move his face in and out of the light, carefully observing the effects of light and shadow, the way in which one might seemingly move like the Devil himself between night and day, the new spaces it opened up for his portrayal of the dying Wardour.

Dickens walked back onto the stage and stood in the brilliant white light. As was the fashion now, the auditorium would be unlit during the performance. He looked down at the pits and was delighted to realise he could see nothing.

He felt a hitherto unknown power and disguise in the white brilliance in which he was bathed, and he realised that what had begun as an amateur theatrical was now going somewhere unexpected and extraordinary. Some of his fellow writers disapproved—Thackeray had said that any vanity is deemed honourable just so long as charity can be named its beneficiary.

Damn Thackeray, thought Dickens. He has posterity. I only have tonight. Damn him! Damn them! Damn them all! He, who was buried, would be resurrected. He, who was dying, encased in pewter, in ice, would now live—if only for a moment—in the blinding white of limelight. And, secure in that dazzle-shaft, with the world beyond finally unseeable, he vowed to imbue Wardour with all he had, to allow his own soul finally to walk naked.

Much to everyone's relief, the opening night saw a full house. Dickens' performance was staggering in its intensity and effect. Watching from backstage, Wilkie Collins was overwhelmed. In the wings he could see hardened carpenters trembling and stagehands weeping, and out in the theatre the audience of thousands swam in tears. Wilkie, eyes also moist, leant across to John Forster.

'It's wonderful,' he whispered. 'But there's something strange, something not right in the performance.'

Forster looked at him, perplexed. His great friend was triumphant, had risen to a new height—what could be better?

'Something terrible,' hissed Wilkie. 'Can you not see it? It is not acting—it is metamorphosis.'

'Come, Wilkie!' cried a stranger's voice. 'It is your cue about to happen.'

And there at their side was a bearded and wretched maniac, not Dickens but Richard Wardour, possessed. He grabbed at Wilkie and, fetching him into his arms, carried him back out onto the stage, where Wilkie was greeted by Maria Ternan as the love of her life, Frank Aldersley, whom she had thought dead.

After the performance, Dickens called on the Ternans

in their dressing room to congratulate them. Ellen Ternan had been struck by the attention and deference shown to this man, of whom she had, on their first meeting, thought so little that she blubbered in front of him. She had heard of him, of course, and she had read *The Pickwick Papers* and some of his other books—who hadn't?—but she had been unprepared for the way the world parted and bowed wherever he went. She felt more important than the royal family once in Manchester. They were lodged in the grand Great Western Hotel; the company was given their very own dining and sitting rooms, where, with her sister Maria, Ellen Ternan had on their first night perhaps a little more brandy than she should, an adventure to which Dickens made a light but pleasing allusion.

After he had left their dressing room, Ellen Ternan noticed on her dressing table a small book Dickens had been carrying in his hand. She looked at it—why, it was a notebook! Perhaps, she thought, Mr Dickens' own notebook! She would not open it; private things, her mother had taught her, were just that. But then, she reasoned, what if it weren't Mr Dickens'? How was one to know without opening it? And so that night she took it with her to bed. Its spine was tight, the pages dun-coloured. It opened like a wounded fledgling hoping to be healed.

There was no name on the inside cover, but Ellen Ternan recognised the handwriting from notes he had scrawled on her script, and so she turned to the next page and the next and the next until she had flicked through the entire book. There were all sorts of lists and titles and queer phrases. '*Undisciplined heart.*' She licked a page. It was plain as pease pudding. '*New ideas for a story have come into my head as I lay on the ground as Wardour, with surprising force and brilliance.*' There was no tale skewering the pieces into a real meal.

She read a few things—she guessed they were for Mr Dickens' next novel. They were mostly gloomy, though there were one or two funny conversations and many curious sentences. '*The wind is rushing after us, and the clouds are flying after us, and the moon is plunging after us, and the wholly wild night is in pursuit of us; but, so far, we are pursued by nothing else.*' Odd names of people. '*Miriam Denial.*' '*Verity Happily.*' '*Mary McQuestion.*' Strange maxims. '*You can have whatever you want, only you discover there is always a price. The question is—can you pay?*' All up, it seemed rather queer, almost boring, and it was a wonder if Mr Dickens could make anything of it and would want it back at all.

She found him the following evening, alone in the manager's office an hour before the performance, at work on his prompt copy.

'Mr Dickens!'

Dickens looked up. He already had on the new make-up he had devised that day to better use the limelight. It accentuated his goatish face.

'Why, you could be Lucifer himself, Mr Dickens!'

He suddenly reared up, threw a finger either side of his forehead, and with a ghastly face gave a roar. Ellen Ternan leapt back squealing, and would have fallen onto a table behind her had not Dickens grabbed her by the wrist.

'I am sorry, Miss Ternan,' he apologised. Ellen Ternan looked down to where her wrist was held in the great author's firm grasp. 'A joke. A poor joke.'

'Nevertheless, even Lucifer does not get the better of me,' said Ellen Ternan. She wrested her wrist free. 'I am an Englishwoman.'

'How remarkable,' said Dickens. 'I mistook you for an Italian vase.'

She no longer knew what to say to one so famous, so instead she just looked him in his eyes. They were dark, and the strange make-up only amplified their blackness. She felt at once frightened by him and drawn to him. In the hope he would take her seriously, she felt obliged to say something serious.

'I liked what you said to Mr Hueffer about the government and the war,' she said, referring to when Dickens had taken exception to a comment made by the manager of the Free Trade Hall about the importance of winning the war in the Crimea. She had to admit, she found him rather handsome. 'About how a highly decorated English general might be a complete fool, but his misadventures will always be a success, most particularly when they are a disaster for which words like gallantry are invented. That did make me laugh.'

Dickens smiled. Ellen Ternan smiled back, and produced from behind her back his notebook, waving it in front of him while shaking her head as though admonishing him.

'Ruin ought be, if ruin must come, ruinously worthwhile,' she said, not knowing this was not playing. She placed the notebook on the dressing table and slid it across to him. Just as she went to withdraw her hand, he reached out and the tips of their fingers touched. Dickens neither picked the book up nor moved his fingers away.

'It is not going well,' said Ellen Ternan. Her body was conscious only of his touch. But this time she did not pull her hand away. She looked up.

'The war,' she said, 'I mean.'

'Wars,' he said, 'rarely do.'

She felt as though lightning were passing through her body and, at the same time, utterly foolish for feeling that way.

'Lady Franklin must be so very grateful. And Mrs Jerrold.'

And having named other women who had secured some form of favour from the great man, Ellen Ternan could not resist the hope that she, too, might find herself part of that company. She was trying to keep her breathing contained. Dickens slowly withdrew his hand and the notebook, and then—but did she imagine it? And if he did do it, she wondered, did he mean anything by it?

For, as he lifted the notebook, he traced the slightest line down her index finger with his own. And where he traced the line, her finger burnt, and there was about that burning something shameful and something wicked and something altogether wonderful.

Dickens talked about the play as if nothing had

happened, but still her finger burnt and burnt and she was unsure if anything had or hadn't happened. And though her burning finger assured her something had, all she knew with certainty was that she wished to stay with him, have him guide her, just be in his company till the day ended and beyond.

He sought her comments on his performance.

She told him it was very powerful, but that if he were to say his lines a little slower and let them breathe with pauses, it might be astonishing. She was not quite sure why he would care to know her thoughts at all, but seeing him look so intently at her, she picked up courage and continued.

'Let your face and hands tell the audience what it is you feel. Pull the people into you, sir, with every movement, pull them in as if you might hug them, and then and only then let your words fire into them like a cannon pressed to the heart. I have known it, sir, that when you hold a moment for so long—*then* count three beyond that before saying anything more—that it can work fulsomely well.'

She didn't quite know what fulsomely meant, but felt it was better that something worked well in a fulsome manner than unsupported by such a brace. As she spoke, she waved her arms and hands about as if in illustration of her argument.

'Miss Ternan,' began Dickens.

'Nell,' she said. 'Everyone calls me Nell.'

'Nell,' he said. 'Very well, then.' And in his imagination he had the overwhelming sense of those same arms, naked, wrapping around his neck, and those same hands rising up through the hair at the back of his head as if about to join in prayer. 'You had better call me Charles.'

She smiled.

'On account of your *Old Curiosity Shop*, sir. Little Nell.'

By the second night, people were being turned away in their hundreds. That afternoon Dickens and Ellen Ternan met for tea in the hotel dining room. Mrs Ternan was to come, but excused herself at the final moment because she had been contacted by an old friend, with whom she had once worked in theatre and who was now married to a cotton magnate.

'A Cottonopolis contessa,' said Ellen Ternan. 'Now there is an invitation no one can say no to!'

And in this way, Ellen Ternan and Charles Dickens were for a third time alone together. Rather than cakes, Ellen Ternan ordered cherries, which the waiter assured her were the finest, all the way from Kent. But neither ate as they talked theatre, about which Ellen had several very funny stories new to him; politics, in which her views were not as disillusioned as those of Dickens, who could see very little prospect of any good arising, but felt the fight for sane progress must never be quit; literature, in which she shared with him a great love of the masters, Fielding and Smollett. Thackeray she enjoyed, but she secretly pleased Dickens—who was frequently beset by that most sincere of literary emotions, jealousy—when she said the great man struck her as a Clydesdale running in the Derby.

Then they laughed about things that had taken place over the last few days, he made many jokes, until, without reason, the conversation froze, and it became as impossible to talk as only a moment before it had been easy. After a silence that neither could fill, he spoke to her in a way that was halting and awkward.

'For a long time I felt I degraded myself, giving in to what life had brought me. These last few days have . . . well, I can see, Nell, I can see I was wrong.'

None of what he said made any sense to Ellen Ternan. More from a sudden nervousness than any appetite, she placed a cherry she had been rolling in her fingers into her mouth, sucked the flesh for a moment as if it were a sweet, and then delicately rolled the still pulpy pit to her lips' edge, took it between thumb and forefinger and dropped it in a bowl.

Dickens stared at that spent stone with its wet threads of red flesh. He envied its good fortune. With a sudden movement, as unexpected to him as it was to her, he scooped the pip up and swallowed it. Looking back up, his eyes caught hers.

She burst out laughing and he joined in, giggling at the absurdity of it. And at that moment he felt no shame, though he wished terribly that he might feel shame, or fear, or at least concern. But to the contrary, he felt intoxicated.

Not long after Ellen Ternan returned to her room, there was a knock at her door and a messenger with an envelope.

Inside it was a card with hotel letterhead and a message in the distinctive hand she now knew as that of Dickens. '*Dear Miss N,*' it began.

> *I wish you to know that you are the last dream of my soul. In my degradation, the sight of you has stirred old shadows that I thought had died out of me. Since I have known you, I have been troubled by a remorse that I thought would never reproach me again, and have heard whispers from old voices impelling me upward that I thought were silent for ever. I have had unformed ideas of striving afresh, beginning anew, shaking off sloth and sensuality, and fighting out the abandoned fight. A dream, all a dream, that ends in nothing and leaves the sleeper where he lay down, but I wish you to know that you inspired it.*
>
> *Burn this card.*
>
> *C.*

Ellen Ternan read and reread the card. She did not burn it. She did not really understand it. It made no more sense than his mysterious words over tea. It confused her and excited her and pressed on her. She knew it meant something, something large and ominous, but what that large and ominous thing was eluded her thinking.

Was this not a personal communication from the most famous writer in all of England addressed to her—Nelly Ternan? And was that not the most marvellous and extraordinary and remarkable thing, and was it not that this most famous writer in England thought her interesting and clever and inspiring?

She held the card close to her chest, longing to run into the room next door and tell Maria, but something warned her against that action. It *was* the most marvellous, extraordinary, remarkable thing—yet instead of telling her sister, she hid the card away at the bottom of her carpet bag. Was it those words 'Burn this card'? She could not say. It was not age; after all, several of her friends—perfectly respectable—had married at fifteen and sixteen, some to men three times their age. No, it was something else. Mr Dickens was married. She hid it—why did she hide it? She did not know, only that doing this, if nothing else, was wise.

That night, Dickens was once again Wardour, and Wardour was even more possessed, demonic, remorseful, redeemed. Once more, he sacrificed himself for love. The sobbing of the front rows could be plainly heard.

As he played the role, Dickens was more than ever determined to behave nobly and selflessly, like Wardour. It could not go on! He must cut himself adrift from Ellen Ternan, no matter the cost, the anguish, the misery, the waking death that would be his life henceforth.

'It was the greatest performance of the play that I could have imagined,' Wilkie told Dickens after. 'You literally electrified the audience.'

He could not know that, as the applause rained down and down at the play's end, a strange sensation grew and grew in Dickens until it was the most terrible fear. He was advancing down a narrow tunnel, through the blackness of that overwhelming noise, to a place from where he would never return.

II

Several months after the Franklins departed, the authorities once more grew concerned about keeping Van Diemen's Land free of black rebellion. This terrifying prospect was embodied in the only native who remained: a twelve-year-old child who had largely ceased to talk and who, in a way she had learnt in Crozier's cabin and refined in the company of the other children at the orphanage, had become absent from her life.

'Some even believe she cast a Satanic spell over the previous Governor,' said Montague, as the new Governor scanned the memorandum recommending Mathinna be sent back to what remained of her exiled people on Flinders Island.

'I am an Anglican,' said the new Governor, throwing sand over his quickly scrawled signature, 'and thus I am relieved of the burden of having to believe in anything.'

———

Since so many others had left them forever, the Wybalenna natives were excited to have one child return. The arrival of Mathinna was an event. They posted lookouts on Flagstaff Hill, they rushed to the beach waving when the sloop berthed, and they began shouting when they saw the ship's tender being lowered with a skinny black child sitting in its bow. They put their arms around her when Mathinna stepped out of the boat. It was like being the black princess of Hobart all over again. It was like the theatre plays that sometimes came to Hobart and to which Lady Jane had taken her. Only now she was both the actor and the audience.

Mathinna showed neither joy nor happiness till she realised no one would make her wear clogs on the pain of beating if she didn't. She took off the heavy pine slippers. The skin of her feet was soft and white and flaky. The ends of her toes looked as if they had been wrapped with wet dough. She scrunched them back and forth in the wet sand of the Wybalenna beach. Behind her, waves roared. The air smelt of tea-tree and salt and life. In front of her, fairy wrens darted in the flotsam, brilliant blue in the glistening bull kelp.

She threw the clogs into a tea-tree grove.

The crowd laughed and roared approval. But she was outside of their excitement and squealing and questions. She had not returned with the albino possum that shat musket balls. She had not come back to them with laughter. She dug her toes further into the sand. She was aware of the gritty rub and rasp of life. But she was a blind woman staring. Shoving her feet deeper and deeper, she knew it was true: she could feel nothing.

After a short time, the excitement of the Wybalenna natives evaporated. They found Mathinna strange. She saw the whites as her kin, not them.

'Mathinna left us,' said Gooseberry, 'and she still gone.'

The girl found the few Aborigines she met on her return dirty, ignorant and indolent. She showed no sign of shock when she discovered the rest were dead, all buried in Robinson's cemetery, and Robinson himself gone to Australia with his tame blacks to bring his protection to the Port Phillip Aborigines.

'Them strangers to me,' she told Dr Bryant, the man who now ran the settlement, in front of several of those she so maligned. 'Just filthy strangers.'

She simply did what she always now did: cast her mind adrift, and very soon it was floating above the cemetery, looking down at the other Aborigines who had taken her there, looking at herself—no longer a beautiful child in beautiful clothes, but now a broken bough of a girl clad in a grubby brown petticoat and ripped blue pullover.

Occasionally the spindly girl said something because she had to, and, floating above, she could understand that she spoke in a manner that was neither white nor black, but in a strange way with strange words that made no sense to anyone. Who was this girl? Why did she talk this way, why this strange wavering voice?

One of the Aborigines, a young man called Walter Talba Bruney, was angry. He was saying he did not understand why this was happening, all this death. He pointed at the graves and yelled into her face, as though it were her fault, as though she might have returned to Wybalenna with some answer. Some message, some explanation, some hope. But she had only a red dress that no longer fitted and that she had taken to wearing as a scarf.

She did not know that Walter Talba Bruney's passion impressed some, and that he thought it might impress her. She didn't move. She didn't care. She understood that none of it meant anything.

'Kill me too, then,' she said.

He had no power over such a girl.

Those not dead numbered fewer than a hundred and were in despair, and still they kept dying. Of a morning the women would walk to the top of Flagstaff Hill and sit there all day, looking at an outline sixty miles south, the distant coastline of their homeland. There, their villages of rotting cupola huts awaited a return that would never happen; their forest glades were filling with saplings, their tracks with scrub, and their hunting plains were being fenced and filled with sheep. They would call to their abandoned ancestors who kept trying to sing them home, so that their own souls would not be lost forever, but there was no answer.

Mathinna did not go to Flagstaff Hill. At first she spent much of her time with the Catechist, Robert McMahon. He was so dirty that Dr Bryant told his wife that if the island ever ran out of provisions, McMahon's shirt could be boiled for the food preserved in its black larded recesses.

'I don't plead laxity and I don't plead stupidity,' McMahon had said to Dr Bryant, in explanation of why he was there. 'I only ask forgiveness.' He kept saying it, as though his original intention of a peaceful, if mediocre, colonial sinecure had given way to complicity in some strange, unseeable crime. It was true that McMahon faced, with Dr Bryant, the grim task of maintaining some sort of order in what the Protector's son had described as a charnel house he was glad to be leaving.

At first McMahon was curious and caring, learnt something of the natives' language and translated some of Scripture into it, but that didn't stop anyone dying and it didn't stop the government cutting and cutting again the annual outlay for the settlement. There was always less food, less clothing, less of everything. In time, Bryant and McMahon resorted to withholding food and contemplated the possibility of shooting some natives to keep them peaceable, but still they provocatively went on dying.

McMahon was dirtier than any black, with an enormous capacity to misquote Scripture at great length, and he seemed at once to side with the blacks as well as to despise them. For Mathinna, he had the added virtue of being unpopular with the natives, which she felt must mean he was a good man. To impress him, she made notes in a diary in his presence, as she had often seen Lady Jane do.

McMahon demanded to see what Mathinna was writing. She showed him, thinking it might raise his opinion of her above that of the other blacks, with whom she had regrettably been lumped. Though she made a great show of writing much, he discovered she in fact wrote very little. He did not know that she saw writing in equal measure as a reward, a show of good behaviour—like washing with soap—and a form of power. If he had, he would have laughed.

Sometimes she copied out Scripture, sometimes advertisements for cottons, horses, soaps or medicines from old *Hobart Town Chronicles*. Taking up her diary, Robert McMahon read aloud:

They should not throw about the soap they have too much the soap is fine thing to wash yourselves with and yet they don't care for it, no they would sooner put on that there red clayey stuff what they have being always used and they like it better than soap to their faces.

Halting only between words slimy with the spittle spume his lips wore along with a corncob pipe, he read on.

Now you see there is none of the good people alive Walter Talba Bruney says that is a good thing Gods thing and them all go to Glory No, I think they dead and gone Walter Talba Bruney say If that when I die let me wake back up in the hunt with plenty kangaroo and emu and no questions No I cannot see my fathers face I dream the trees know everything and tell me everything No I cannot see him the trees I dream know everything.

Robert McMahon threw her diary into the fire.

——

Three years passed. Then came the summer of fire. Stories of its never-ending nature, of how it was destroying vast tracts of the far distant Australian mainland interior, arrived with a brig that emerged out of a December sunrise with Robinson's tame blacks, returned from their time with the Protector on the mainland. They had broken free of Robinson and run with the Australian Aborigines, telling them to kill the white man or be killed. They had shot stock-keepers, looted shepherds' huts, burnt houses, killed two whalers. The white men had caught and hanged Timmy, they had caught and hanged Pevay, but the other six natives—three women and three men—had, through the Protector's intervention, been saved and returned to Wybalenna.

These women were different from the women who sat on Flagstaff Hill. They taught the other women a new dance, the devil dance. Of a day Mathinna kept on with a new diary, but of an evening she watched the devil dance around the big campfire. For a time she sought to persuade the returned women that their ways were uncouth and uncivilised, but at night she listened in wonder as the old women told their stories of all that they had seen—at the hands of the sealers and whalers, the government men and the missionary men. For they had discovered something remarkable: the world was not run by God but by the Devil.

The world was hennaed by a smoke haze that never ended, that brought the sky low and softened every view of the bleak and fantastic hills into something uncertain. The sun was no longer solid and sure but red and shaking.

By day the air was full of the acrid smell of fires hundreds of miles distant, but the nights filled with the sound and shrieks of devil dancing. The evening she finally stood up to join in, Mathinna was speckled with charred leaves and blackened fronds that had been carried by the wind from the Australian mainland, to finally eddy and drift to earth at Wybalenna.

She had grown friendly with Walter Talba Bruney, whom she found odder than herself. He was twenty-two, yet to run to fat, still handsome, and regarded by the few Aborigines as one of their big men. Walter Talba Bruney was certain of many things, having been educated by the Protector, of whom he had once been a favourite, and was seemingly at ease with both the whites and his own people. Son of a Ben Lomond chieftain, he had magical powers. He could, for example, write.

His writing was so powerful that it had come to be regarded as a form of sorcery. He had threatened, for a time, to put the names of those old people who would not take to the Protector's ways in the *Flinders Island Chronicle*, a single handwritten sheet of which he was editor, writer, draftsman, proprietor and promoter, a threat that brought on terror and, with it, a short-lived compliance.

The day after she first devil-danced, Mathinna had swum for crayfish and abalone, and Walter Talba Bruney and she had cooked them on a small fire on the beach and, after, had lain in the sand. Then came a dusk of stories, of what she had seen, the madness and strangeness of white people.

Walter Talba Bruney told her how he was not scared

of the whitefellas and he had ideas, and his ideas, once those of his white teachers, were now changing. He would get land back. They would live on their own wheat and potatoes, their own muttonbirds and eggs and sheep. They did not need whitefellas ruling them. He would write to the Queen. It was the hour before midnight that Robert McMahon discovered Mathinna on the moonlit beach giving to Walter Talba Bruney what had been taken from her by another.

Enraged, he thrashed them both with a thin tea-tree cane he kept specially for the purpose. He wanted Walter Talba Bruney to think about God and Hell and punishment, and to help, he imprisoned him for seventeen days. To rescue her otherwise lost and damned soul, McMahon made Mathinna his maid.

In his home he spoke in voices. He told Mathinna she was Chosen. He beat her on an almost daily basis. He flogged her at every opportunity for her failings, the one activity that seemed to bring him pleasure. When blood at last ran down her black back, he would begin talking, his speech as measured as his stroke.

'You understand,' he said, as he diligently continued to flog her, 'she was in her nineteenth year and with child. She lived in the practice of every Christian and womanly virtue and died in the full assurance of a better life beyond the grave.'

It was, Mathinna understood, another form of the catechism.

The women who had brought back the devil dance had

also brought back fresh supplies of red ochre for ceremony. They refused to work in the gardens unless they were paid, or to clean their houses unless they got better clothes. They urged the men to stand up. They told the women they must fight back.

Jesus was a trick of the Devil, they said. The Devil ran the world. There was no light at the end, no redemption, no justice. God, heaven, whitefella talk—all tricks of the Devil. There was no black dreaming, no white heaven, only that bugger, the Devil, buggering everything.

They had lived it, they had seen it; there was no argument that they could not shoot down with the terrible argument of their wretched lives. Maybe up there in the stars was the hunt that never ended, which the old fellas talked about. But you would have to fight to get there. Go with the Devil, enjoy the Devil—what else is there? You think the Devil lose? When the Devil ever lose? You tell me. You tell me when the Devil not ruin your life? You dance with him, you enjoy the Devil. Because he going to take us all soon, no matter. No matter what.

And then they would laugh: a terrible laugh that joined with the quickening scent of bull kelp, an overwhelming smell of wet sex that arose from the thick leathery horns of serpentine green, hundreds of feet long, which washed up everywhere along the coast. The scent was blowing up from the beach on the westerly wind the night Mathinna silently laid out long, thin blades of dead grass-tree along the windward side of the Catechist's house, as patiently as if she were stitching petticoats at the orphanage.

She remembered the pages of her diary yellowing, her dreams of trees curling and transforming into ash in the Catechist's fire, and she knew what she must do. She laid one layer horizontally, so the fire would bed and be harder to extinguish, and over it she thatched vertically, so the flames would catch the wind and rise speedily. Then she went away and devil-danced, and when the campfire had ebbed to little more than coals and all the blackfellas were weary and all the whites asleep, she made a firebrand out of a tea-tree stick and bound bracken.

When Robert McMahon ran from the burning conflagration, alive and unscorched and wearing only a filthy shirt, to catch Mathinna throwing a pile of bracken on the burning house, he did not ask if she was guilty and she did not pretend she wasn't. He made her kneel, bound her hands and flogged her with his tea-tree stick.

The few men left with magic cursed him. It did no good. He thrashed Mathinna all the more. He was as imperishable as ants, and no matter how much you stamped on him he always came back. He survived flames. He survived curses, incantations, the pointed bones of the dead. He did not survive being thrown overboard a mile out from Big Dog Island by his native boatman, but still the Aborigines kept dying. Robinson's cemetery filled with ever more Aboriginal corpses.

Some whites worried about the possible extinction of the race, others fervently prayed for it; but all concurred as to the melancholy and listlessness that now prevailed amongst the formerly warlike and active people. Mathinna would awake screaming. The old people asked her to tell them what her nightmares were. There was nothing to tell.

'No good dreams any more,' she said, her one solace from her time in Hobart Town vanished. She did not like to say her father never came to see her, because she did not wish to shame him and understood there must be a reason and that she must be it. She did not say she could no longer remember her father's face.

Finally, when there were only forty-seven Van Diemonian natives left, when it was apparent that they no longer posed any threat, when it was clear it was costing too much money to keep the last remnants of their race in the misery to which they had grown accustomed, the new Governor decreed they could finally be returned and live in worse misery in their home country. They were interred at Oyster Cove, south of Hobart Town, in some crumbling slab huts once used as convict barracks. There they subsisted on rum and a government ration of two pounds of meat a day.

The six surviving native children, Mathinna among them, were sent to St John's Orphanage. They arrived there in the evening. She held her face in her hands, as if she were unsure that both it and she were still there, and looked skywards. Through the cracks between her fingers a silver light fell.

'Towterer,' she whispered.

There is a crack in all things, she thought. She was fifteen years old and she had survived by clinging to the smallest things.

———

After six months at the orphanage, Mathinna was sent to work for a seamstress, Mrs Dellacorte, in a street off Salamanca. The black princess was, for a short time, an attraction in her own right, a celebrity Mrs Dellacorte recognised for its commercial worth from the beginning. The seamstress, a faded beauty who favoured red wigs, and whose looks had retreated behind a veil of white lead powder to form a ghost mask, made her money not from dress repair of a day, but a sly grog shop of a night. It was here that Mathinna was expected to work, fetching jugs of rum and lemon, of gin and sugar for American whalers and Maori sealers, for redcoats off for a night and the occasional old lag who had somehow scrounged enough for another drink.

'You can take whatever you want,' said the seamstress. 'Just don't take me down.'

Mathinna understood that meant she, too, could indulge in the hot pleasure of rum and tea spiced with cinnamon, for which she quickly acquired a strong appetite.

Mrs Dellacorte and her black pug dog, Beatrice, ruled the taproom with an icy ruthlessness. Whoever irritated the mistress or her dog were no longer spoken of or with, and a second offence saw you thrown out. Beatrice, when not in the lap of Mrs Dellacorte or wandering around tabletops licking food off plates with a hideous tongue of reptilian length and dexterity, sat on a filthy lambskin at the entrance of a long dark hall, wheezing worse than a dying consumptive.

In a darkened parlour was Mrs Dellacorte's prize possession, set on a rammed dirt floor: a billiard table with one broken leg resting on a butcher's old chopping block. Hung above the fireplace, a portrait of Mrs Dellacorte as a young woman of some beauty looked across at the table, as if in a final plea—for the hope of something better? forgiveness? love? For Mrs Dellacorte lived in a loveless universe, the horror of which she kept at bay with what lay strewn over the billiard table's worn felt: mementos and keepsakes of her late lover, a womanising spendthrift who claimed to be of Hapsburgian lineage.

There were scabbards without swords, compasses without needles, even an astrolabe with a bent alidade, along with several newspapers written in a strange, unreadable script, which Mrs Dellacorte said was Hungarian. She claimed these recorded her husband's feats of arms in several forgotten wars. All this was shown to any guest she considered of consequence, to establish herself as a woman of position as well as passion. The relics were, however, out of bounds to everyone else.

Whatever transaction passed between the orphanage and the seamstress, who was meant to provide for Mathinna until she was eighteen, none passed between the seamstress and Mathinna. She scrounged scraps and stole drinks and, receiving no pay, took to getting pennies and bread for what Sir John had stolen. She set no store by it. It wasn't pleasant—but then, what in her life was? It was the Devil's world, after all. She even sometimes took an odd comfort in it: it can be no worse than this, she would tell herself as they slobbered and grunted and shoved.

But it could, and the worst was when the memories crowded together, of her people, their kindnesses, their laughter, the singing and dancing around the campfire. In between, she went to the Queen's Domain, where she caught green and red rosella parrots and sold them to those who liked eating them in pies.

She noticed a weeping between her legs and a general itching. She realised she had the pox. Since just about everyone else she knew did too, it seemed as unremarkable, if as annoying and occasionally painful, as the lice that also beset her. A friend gave her a phial of quicksilver to drink. She vomited, her nails all fell out, and after a time the weeping and itching disappeared.

Mostly she longed for sleep and its sweet oblivion. The moment she reached her cot and found her way under a possum-skin rug, she felt safe.

One night a very tall, very skinny old man in a splendid coat came into the widow's back room. He had, another girl told Mathinna, made his money speculating, using a small inheritance to buy a half-share in a whaling expedition that had multiplied into several whaling ships. On seeing her, he smiled. He had only talked to her for a few minutes before she insisted that if he wanted her, he would have to pay like the other men. His smile halted, and he opened his bony fingers to reveal the incomprehensible sight of a guinea coin.

It was a night of sleet, and they went not to her normal workplace, a stall left empty for the purpose in the stables, but stole into Mrs Dellacorte's slightly less chill parlour of sacred memory. But when Mathinna went to pull her skirts up, he halted her, sat her down, and gave her another guinea coin, along with a question.

'Miss Mathinna—do you not remember me?'

Only when he fished out a button accordion from his saddle bag did she recognise him. It was Mr Francis Lazaretto. As he played *The Ballad of the Cyprus Brig*, his voice captured her one last time. When he slowed the song, and strange, sad, sweet sounds came from that battered little bellows, she span this way and that in slow evocation of the joyful dancing his music had once inspired in her. When he went to leave, he spoke just one sentence that meant nothing to her.

'More forms of consummation than one.'

And at that moment the door opened, and in strode a panting black pug, long tongue lolling, followed by Mrs Dellacorte. She took just one look at the black girl sitting on the billiard table who had so obviously profaned her most precious shrine, and as Mathinna scampered out behind Francis Lazaretto, Mrs Dellacorte told her not to bother coming back.

While riding in his carriage to a meeting with Pedder to discuss an enticing business proposal—a large pastoral run in the burgeoning new colony of Port Phillip—Montague saw a young Aboriginal woman staggering towards him.

'I hardly recognised her, she was that changed—and none of it for the better,' Montague later told Pedder.

He had suffered a stroke. One side of his mouth drooped with a palsy and his words slurred. 'Her face was bloated and bleeding from some thrashing or fall, while her body seemed all sticks.'

'I'm told she wanders the town, drinking in the gutters,' Pedder replied.

'I pulled the carriage blind down, just so,' said Montague—here he leant forward and pretended to be spying out a narrow strip of glass—'well, you understand.' They laughed at the idea of the wretch embarrassing him. 'But here was the queerest thing—she spotted me and just smiled! Can you believe it? It was as though everything for her was utterly real and at the same time without any foundation—including me!—and somehow this seemed to keep her, who is constantly humiliated, jeered at by any who see her, who I am told routinely has mud or stones hurled at her, in this smiling state of some deranged superiority.'

'I have seen it myself,' said Pedder. 'She roams the streets as if it were all a dream.'

But something about Mathinna's fall and the way she now deported herself troubled both men. It was hard to know whether her seeming acceptance was submission or simple-mindedness or the most profound revolt, a contempt greater than any visited on her by pox-raddled redcoats, shepherds or ticket-of-leave men.

'She was many things,' said Montague, lost with his own thoughts. 'She was never simple-minded.' An exclamation mark of drool fell from his lip.

At times Mathinna could seem naturally haughty, as if her peculiar history had indeed bequeathed that very majesty she had once been promised, as though from her full height of five foot four she had seen everything there was of people and somehow now stood above them, aware of their failings but without judgement. Some in Hobart Town regarded it as nigger stupidity, others as arrogance; some said it was just the grog, others recalled older tales of her witchery. She was easily reviled, laughed at and sometimes spat upon, but the thought of her played uneasily on people's minds.

She continued trading her body, because, along with a little writing and the quadrille, it was what she had learnt and finally come to understand as her only possibility for survival. Loathsome as Mrs Dellacorte's establishment had been, it had offered a dry cot and palliasse, a fire, and even if the food was bad, there was always enough of it, and the worst men were thrown out if they roughed up a girl.

Now the sailors and old lags and soldiers took her ever more drunkenly, hopelessly, violently, painfully, in anger and with tears, with their rotten broken mouths and foul breath tonguing hate and begging forgiveness, rarely curious and generally desperate to be rid of her the moment they were done. That, if little else, suited her.

Besides, she understood that what she sold was not herself but a shell, from which at some point she would be freed. A few knew her story, or enough to taunt her, but they never understood that it was not her they were abusing with their vile words and rough fingers and abject bodies, because she was not there in that odd jumble and tug and hitch of two bodies in a muddy lane or the bush behind the town.

'She was the Governor's pet piccaninny princess, you know, all pearly smile and tarry flashness,' she heard a voice say one dark evening as she staggered up Cat and Fiddle Lane. 'But now she's lost her looks.'

'Grown into them, more like it,' said a second voice, reedy and wretched. 'She's just another black ape now.'

Realising they were standing just around the corner, Mathinna halted.

'A Chartist, more like it,' laughed the first voice. 'There for all.'

Though Mathinna did not understand exactly what was meant by this conversation, she understood it was something she could not even shape into thought: that, with those words, something undeniable had been denied her.

'Jesus, he bleed like a blackfella,' she said later that night, to a sawyer taking her too roughly from behind.

'God's free,' he said. 'You're not.'

Nor was she, but her price was quickly dropping. Her hair was coming out in so many hanks she tied what remained of her red scarf around it, most of her teeth had gone or were going, and her skin was scabby. She traded her raddled flesh for johannas, mohurs, rupees, pieces of Spanish dollars, cartwheel pennies and Degraves' despised Tassie shillings when she was lucky, and for pieces of pickled pork and long swigs of whatever when she was desperate. Sometimes that was several times a night out the back of various grog shops, occasionally it was bartered quickly off the track that led from Hobart Town through the hills and down D'Entrecasteaux Channel to Oyster Cove, where the handful of survivors of Wybalenna, with whom she spent more and more of her time, were now interred.

She stopped trapping birds. She drank more. It was apparent to her—albeit in a dull and confused way that she found beyond any words she knew, either of her own tongue or of English—that other people seemed to revel and delight with purpose in this life and this world. Ma'am existed for a reason, for hundreds of reasons with names like Education, Advancement, Civilisation. The convicts longed to escape, the soldiers to become settlers, the settlers to make more money. Even the old people at Oyster Cove held the hope of return to the land and the ancestors, if not in this life then in the next.

Mathinna yearned for some similar fire to live by, but in the meantime made do with what helped her endure, with what enabled her to survive. Mostly that was drink. Sometimes she still held her hands over her eyes and looked for the cracks of light. But less and less. More and more she drank towards the darkness.

George Augustus Robinson called in to Oyster Cove on his way home to England, to say a final farewell to what remained of those he had protected. He was mystified that they had little to say to him, and there was no excitement at his visit. He had been particularly interested to meet with Mathinna and see what had become of the experiment of the black princess, but all he met with were sorry rumours.

He reflected on the strangeness of this final meeting many years later in the town of Bath, to which he had retired, as he closed a large trunk full of his assembled papers detailing his strange history of encounters with the savages of Australia and Van Diemen's Land. Robinson had hoped to make something of them—a book, celebrity, honours, money. That most elusive accolade, greatness. No one was interested. Nor, ultimately, he had discovered, was he. His major cause for regret was not holding out for more money when he brought in the last of the natives. Money, money, money, and what money can make of life!

His ambitions, like his body, were collapsing. He found balance difficult. He hoped for a brass plaque to be attached to his house after his death. He was no longer sure how best to lobby for, or even obliquely suggest, such an honour on the ever-rarer occasions he met the few who paraded themselves as powerful in the old Regency spa town. What was he commemorating? His thoughts were mist. He heard strange chanting. Saw a naked man dancing between the stars and the earth. Remembered rivers, a dark child at his door, fingers greasy with sawing. He awoke early on the eighteenth of October 1866 and, rolling his head to one side in his warm bed, he looked at an autumnal light, red and diffuse, softly falling through a window. He felt a great serenity wash over him, his body peacefully stretched out, and, secure in the knowledge he had been a good man who had helped many others, he died.

12

SEATS FOR THE FINAL NIGHT were impossible to procure. People who had come by train from as far away as London were begging ticket touts for pity. Lady Jane had been luckier. After she missed seeing the play in London because of fundraising engagements elsewhere, she had been delighted to receive an invitation for that evening's performance, along with a delightful letter, from Mr Dickens himself.

Travelling into the heart of Manchester that uncharacteristically hot August morning felt to Lady Jane like descending into the cone of Vesuvius. The light was ochre and the sweaty air tasted of sulphur; iron horseshoes and the iron wheels of omnibuses, coaches, wagons and drays were thundering all around her, a cacophony of noise like ten thousand smithies. And like a spectator on a volcano, she was enjoying these marvellous sensations of a most modern city when her landau carriage, taking a side road to avoid the flyblown corpse of a horse, became caught up in a funeral cortege.

She travelled the world now, her vengeance on her husband's obstinacy applauded as noble grief, her part as loyal widow having emancipated her from men and allowing her freedoms few other women could imagine. Her life, as a studied melancholy, she savoured. To admit to happiness would have been inappropriate, but as her cursing driver sought a way around, she believed herself to be fulfilled.

Craning her head, she could see it was a child's hearse, half-sized, white-painted, brass-railed and white ostrich feather-plumed. Inside lay a toy-sized coffin. Water from the melting ice packed beneath that small, sad box dripped down the hearse's jolting rear. As those beads of water splashed on the street's hot cobbles, vanishing into steam, Lady Jane found her pleasant thoughts evaporating.

'Faster,' she yelled to the landau's driver. 'Get me there faster.'

At the Grand Western Hotel, Ellen Ternan's spirits were also not what they had been. All day she had the sense Dickens was avoiding her. She worried that she had lost his respect, she cursed herself for becoming too familiar. Meanwhile Maria Ternan had woken unwell, and by the afternoon her cold was so bad her voice had gone. Against this loss Maria could do nothing, and it was clear that she would not be able to perform that night as Wardour's love, Clara Burnham.

An hour and a half before the curtain went up, Ellen Ternan received a terse note from Dickens saying Mr Hueffer had found a local actress to fill her role, freeing her to take her sister's place in the lead. She burst into tears, not knowing whether it was from relief or terror, or both.

Though each evening had seen an ever more extraordinary performance from Dickens, even the cast were unprepared for the intensity and emotion of Dickens' acting that final evening.

'It's as though it's no longer a play, but life itself,' said Wilkie to Forster, as they waited in the wings for their calls.

'I'm simply glad the folly's finishing,' replied Forster, without turning. 'If this goes on any longer, he'll end up more lost than Sir John.'

Seated in the best box in the house, Lady Jane gasped in shock with the rest of the audience when, in the concluding act, Dickens made his last appearance as the dying Wardour. She had to raise a cologne-scented handkerchief to her nose, for the stench of sweaty wool and animal odour rising from the heated crowd below seemed to worsen with each sensational development in the play. He had become a terrible being, eyes glaring like a wild animal's, long grey hair and beard matted, his clothes no more than piteous rags.

'Who is it you want to find?' asked Ellen Ternan. 'Your wife?'

Dickens shook his head wildly.

'Who, then? What is she like?'

On stage, Dickens was allowed finally to stare into her eyes, to take in her cheeks, her nose, her lips, and he could not stop staring. Little by little, the hoarse, hollow voice he affected for the part softened.

'Young,' he said, 'with a fair, sad face, with kind tender eyes. Young and loving and merciful,' he now cried out, not to the audience but to Ellen Ternan, his voice no longer Wardour's but strangely his own. 'I keep her face in my mind, though I can keep nothing else. I must wander, wander, wander—restless, sleepless, homeless—till I find her! Over the ice and snow, tramping over the land, awake all night, awake all day, wander till I find her!'

Lady Jane, looking down from her box, was thinking how, like Clara Burnham, she had demonstrated the purity and virtue of her love. Yet far from making her feel vindicated with her life, instead of thinking nobly of Sir John, the play was taking her back to those final years in Van Diemen's Land. There was such a wrongness about something, such a terrible wrongness, that she feared she might scream.

Dickens turned and sensed the huge audience out there in the darkness. Wardour had ceased to exist and was drifting away with the steam rising from his hot body. Yet he felt the heat of the crowd wanting something more. Though he did not know what it was, he knew he would keep giving it to them until there was nothing left and only death remained, death that had chased him here, death that was eating him even there on the stage. He suddenly fell to the floor—the audience gasped, someone shrieked in horror. Ellen Ternan knelt down and gently rolled his head into her lap.

He could feel her thighs beneath his neck as she cradled him, he could feel the white light envelop them at last as she wrapped him in her arms, and he wanted to stay that way, in her arms and in that light, forever.

Watching through his thick spectacles, Wilkie found himself not simply moved, but astonished as Wardour, now dying in Clara Burnham's arms, finally recognises her as his long-lost love, for whom he has sacrificed everything so that her love, Frank Aldersley, might live. Wilkie had never witnessed anything like it in his life.

Ellen Ternan was looking at Dickens, shaking her head, biting her lips; and, to his amazement, Wilkie could see that she was weeping, not stage tears, but a heartfelt sobbing. In the rows, scores of people were weeping with her. Handkerchief clasped tightly to her face, Lady Jane, too, felt the emotion rising in her as an inexorable panic. Far below, she saw, as if through water, a murky orphanage courtyard and, standing alone within it, a bedraggled child staring back at her.

'You,' said Dickens, shakily.

Lady Jane was leaning down, the audience was coming forward, all craning to better watch and hear. They were like a living being, a single animal, waiting, ready. Dickens realised he was no longer speaking to a script, but that the script was—improbably, inexorably, inescapably— describing his soul.

'You,' he said again, this time louder, for he wanted to fill his mouth with her, he wanted to lose himself in Ellen Ternan's breasts, to bury himself in her belly, to bite her thighs, to be rid of all that being still and alone made him fear. He was panting. His terror was absolute. He was shaking violently, his voice trembling, his words now revelations to him. '*It was always you!*'

'Don't,' said Ellen Ternan, his Nell, saying words that neither Dickens nor Wilkie had ever scripted; then, realising her error, she shook her head. And as her body was seized with a most terrifying presentiment of its destiny, she tried to retreat into her lines, mumbling and confusing them in a way that was mistaken for acting.

But Dickens was pulling her into him, into some strange and terrible new fate, and she was unable to stop falling. She was terrified for them both. She looked around desperately, but everywhere outside the halo of light defining the two of them together was darkness. *The wholly wild night is in pursuit of us; but, so far, we are pursued by nothing else.* The other cast members gathered around. The men reverently uncovered their heads. The end was near; they all saw it now.

'Kiss me, my sister, kiss me before I die!'

His words were firing into her heart like a cannonade without end. Ellen Ternan leant over him and kissed his forehead. She kissed him not simply because it was in the script but because there was an inexorable logic to her kissing him that she struggled against but could not deny. *The question is—can you pay?* She could see now that it was a novel contained in his notebook, only she had not understood until that moment that she was its unwritten heart.

He could feel her lips on his brow, he could feel the immense human tensing of the darkened audience, a black void that radiated some energy that allowed him to live a little longer. He could feel it, feel them, willing him on. He had come here by chance, coincidences were bringing him to his destiny, and yet, as in his stories, he knew there were no coincidences in this world, that the purpose of everything is ultimately revealed, be it a savage's skull or Sir John lost in ice floes or he, Dickens, lost until this moment. He had thought he would have to drag himself in a strange waking sleep through the rest of a life that had become a strange torture. But perhaps it was not so.

'What is it?' asked Dickens, with words Ellen Ternan had never heard before, unscripted words. She looked at him in shock, not knowing what was happening. 'The way we are denied love,' he continued, and she, along with the audience, could hear how hard it was for him to say these words. 'And the way we suddenly discover it being offered us, in all its pain and infinite heartbreak. The way we say no to love.'

He never saw Lady Jane, white-faced, abruptly stand, turn and leave her box. Outside, in her rush to get away from the theatre, she accidentally trod in a gutter gouted with something foul and thick. She dropped her handkerchief and her nose and mouth were overwhelmed by the foul effluvia of the city, heat-leavened and wind-stirred: the wet sewage flowing through the streets and the dry dust of horse dung blowing in the air, the caustic filth of a thousand tanneries, workshops and factories, the stench of a million unwashed bodies.

Lady Jane felt lost, felt that she might vomit. It occurred to her that perhaps one only exists in those who love you. She could not find a landau or even a hansom cab. Had she said no to love, that day she looked down into the courtyard? She called out for a cab, called out louder, but none came. And if you turn away from love, did it mean you no longer existed? Did she? She felt as lost and dead as the silky soot that eddied around her. She was calling louder and louder, but still nobody came.

Inside, the only sound that could be heard was the slow puff and wheeze of the gigantic bellows working hard to sustain the burning limelight, as though that one pale fire were breathing for the two thousand mesmerised audience who remained.

'Don't die,' said Ellen Ternan.

His head lay in her lap, her tears were falling on him like rain, and the universe was flowing into him, he was open to everything, it was an immense thought, a terrifying feeling, something at once outside of himself that had now entered him, a thing both wicked and exhilarating. It was as though he had awoken startled from a dream. He had survived. He felt as if he were coming down from a mountain, that the snow drifts were thinning and then giving way to grasslands, that a great green valley beckoned before him, a space so immense and free he felt himself gasping contemplating it. On and on he walked. The air was sweet, and breathing felt like drinking water on a hot day. He was coming home. It made no sense. It was beyond understanding. He was being held by her, feeling her draw breath. He was tasting her tears. The sound of sobbing from the darkness was unbearable.

'Please don't die,' begged Ellen Ternan.

His cheek pressed against her uncorseted belly. He could feel its softness pulsing in and out. He could not know that within a year his marriage would be ended. That in the thirteen years of life left to him, he would be faithful to Ellen Ternan, but that theirs would be a hidden and cruel relationship. That his writing and his life would change irrevocably. That things broken would never be fixed. That even their dead baby would remain a secret. That the things he desired would become ever more chimerical, that movement and love would frighten him more and more, until he could not sit on a train without trembling. He was smelling her, hot, musty, moist.

'Nelly?' whispered Dickens.

And at that moment, Dickens knew he loved her. He could no longer discipline his undisciplined heart. And he, a man who had spent a life believing that giving in to desire was the mark of a savage, realised he could no longer deny wanting.

13

'WE'VE GIVEN DEATH THE SLIP,' said Walter Talba Bruney. 'But for how long?'

Walter Talba Bruney was a drunk now, and fat and morbid with it. He was only in his late twenties but looked far older. The war had ended, but another war went on and on inside Walter Talba Bruney and it would not let him go. When he was drunk, he was angry with God. When he was sober, he prayed to God to help him get drunk. When he was drunk again, he shouted that if he had a chance, he would get a spear and spear God good, teach him a lesson.

About God Mathinna had no particular opinion—perhaps, as she sometimes told her fellow rum drinkers around the fire, it was because she was high church. But she told Walter Talba Bruney she hated him talking about death.

'All blackfellas die at Wybalenna,' said Walter Talba Bruney, ignoring her. 'We think, come back to our country and we be good and healthy. But we come back here and we keep dying. Devil in us. Devil killing us. God killing us. Why God and the Devil want to work together?'

There were five of them drinking rum and sugar that night: two other natives and Burly Tom, a one-time whaler who had of late been living by mending nets, but who later denied ever being there.

Mathinna swung the conversation to dresses they were now wearing in London, and, though she knew she was only repeating what she had heard years before, she tried to lead the conversation as she had seen Lady Jane lead her soirées, introducing a topic and then turning to someone else for their opinion. Yet when she tried to look her companions directly in the eye, Mathinna realised this wasn't Government House but Ira Bye's sly grog shop—an earthen-floor split-timber hut of two rooms at North West Bay—that it wasn't a soirée and they were anything but society, just stinking no-good stupid blackfellas. She wished she had the Widow Munro's bamboo cane to hold under their chins until they did look back at her, these no-good, good for nothing savages who knew nowt.

And because, as well as a direct gaze, she had in her time at Government House absorbed the idea of example to one's lowers, and because it made the point—to herself as much as to them—that she was somebody, Mathinna talked about the new dances that season in London, though her knowledge here, too, was both hopelessly inadequate and entirely out of date. When she asked Gooseberry what she thought, she just cackled into her cracked china cup, and, not really knowing anything about the whites' new dances, Mathinna turned to the one subject about which she could manifest some authority: why she would like to hunt foxes, something that offered a union of her heritage with her upbringing.

'We been treated shamefully, worse than the old people in the bush,' said Walter Talba Bruney. 'And them savages not good Christian people like us, them just savages who never learnt nothing.' He was mumbling now, and then he had another drink and changed his mind. He felt God was back on his side now, but he couldn't understand why He didn't help more. When Walter Talba Bruney looked up at Mathinna, she saw there were tears in the slits that were left for eyes in his big puffy face and in one tear was caught a flailing louse.

Mathinna knew Walter Talba Bruney now had a wife, and he had tried being respectable, but the government had taken his sheep when they left Flinders Island and now he wanted them back, and moreover he wanted land, and they wouldn't give him anything unless he swore off drink, but, sensing this was just one more lie, he drank all the more.

'We know whitefellas just us, blackfellas when we die we reborn with white skin. But why . . .' He was lost now, somewhere between God and Jesus and savages and civilisation and all their impending deaths and the curious, terrible, impossible certainty they would be reborn as unthinking as a white. 'Why,' he said again. 'Why?'

'I no a savage or slave,' said Mathinna. 'Them no-good lazy blackfellas, they disgust me. I marry a whitefella, you watch, you see, I be big lady.'

'Why you drink with us then if you a white lady?' said Walter Talba Bruney, seemingly startled back into conversation. 'You better be drinking with them.'

But Mathinna drank with Walter Talba Bruney because, other than a few blue gin riders, no one else would. For all that they annoyed each other, the Aborigines shared something so obvious that it sometimes evaded them, as they sought in the rise and fall of their chipped cups and rusty tin mugs, in the merge of their old and new worlds, some answer to who they were and who they might yet be.

Whoever she drank with, Mathinna drank more and more. Which was why—when Walter Talba Bruney walked with her down that dark track from Ira Bye's through the forest, where the setting moonlight was lost in the blackness of the great trees' canopy—she grew angry. It was not that he then hurt her in his entry, nor his excuses that she was not wet or willing or pretty enough any more to deserve any payment, or his nonsense that it was she who should be paying him for such pleasure. It was simply that he refused to give her the half-bottle of rum he had promised in exchange.

That was why she argued with him. It was why, when he yelled back, she spat at him. It was why, when he hit her, she hit him. But when he forced her head down into the puddle, crying out that she could drink this then, there was nothing she could do, try as she might.

All around her were trees older than knowing. If you held your face to their taut mossy bark, you could hear it all. It passed understanding. It defied words and spoke in dreams. She was flying through wallaby grass, her body no longer a torment but a joy. Soft threads of fine grass feathering beads of water onto her legs. The earth was her bare feet, wet and mushy in winter, dry and dusty in summer.

Mathinna managed to lift her head out of the puddle once. Walter Talba Bruney slipped the filthy red scarf from her hair down onto her throat, and twisted its greasy loop into an inescapable garrotte. The track in front of her shuddered. Time and the world were not infinite, and all things end in dirt and mud. She finally saw her father's face. Long, with a slightly bent nose and a kind mouth, it was, she realised with rising terror, as she felt herself being forced back into the wet void, the face of death.

Walter Talba Bruney walked through what remained of the night, returning to a world of light, of children laughing, of horses serenely eating grass, of people who had things to do and lives to live. As dawn broke, he passed an ox driver resting with his beast, and as his home drew close, he came upon a sight that reminded him of his beloved Bible and made him smile: a lamb lost on a road.

Garney Walch stood a moment longer in front of the

ox, warming his hands in the steaming breath billowing from the beast's wet-ringed nostrils. Then he, his ox and sled moved on. His path took him along a clifftop that overlooked the D'Entrecasteaux Channel and its fishing boats and led down into a small valley, where he was to help a farmer and his convict labourer build a barn.

They started the morning selecting dead trees that had barrels straight and true enough for good poles, and then set to work. After felling the trees and stripping their trunks of bark and branches, Garney Walch had his ox haul the poles to a small meadow glistening with so many wet spiders' webs that it seemed veiled in a sticky gossamer. The hoar frost on the long grass was melting to a sparkling dew, and all things, including the men and the ox, steamed in the winter sun as they worked, and all things seemed to have a place.

A mile away, an old lag waded out on a small rocky reef, shivering and cursing and happy in his pursuit. He emptied a dog's leg from a hessian bag into a wicker lobster pot and, carefully choosing his point at the drop-off where a large amount of bull kelp rose, lowered the pot with a long line of hemp rope. And so the sun rose, birds sang, men worked, boats sailed by, and life went on.

A dazzling sunburst of light, ruby gold in colour and warm on the flesh, burst through the eucalypts and found the three men: the farmer, who was worried about his wife, pregnant with their fourth child; the convict, who was hoping to find a wife once free; and Garney Walch, who carried his grief for a daughter lost to typhoid twenty years before as a stone in his belly. The men worked with few words around the fallen trees, rolling, chocking, measuring, sawing, until at last they had nine good poles.

They loaded the sled, three poles a trip from the paddock to the homestead, and before each trip Garney Walch patted the ox on its muzzle and seemed to be sharing a joke with it. He was unexpectedly gentle with such a beast, as though the burden of the logs were equally borne by both.

The sun swung its low winter course, the men slowly divested themselves of coats and worsted shirts, till they laboured only in trousers and dirty undershirts, and when the sun had risen as high as it would get and the men felt no longer stale and putrid but fresh and good, they halted. While the convict got a fire going with the oily spikes of grass-trees, Garney Walch produced some cold hoggets' necks from his sugarbag. The farmer had bread and salt, and they moved two of their poles to form seats around the fire and ate their cold hogget and bread with relish, then washed it down with black tea sweetened with the farmer's plum jam, and talked happily of how well they lived.

After lunch they returned to their labour. As each pole was set in its hole and then the earth rammed into place around it, the men rejoiced. The barked poles were the colour of gnawed bones, dull white with vivid ochre streaks, and the way they stood in odd pattern, both part of and separate from the world around, filled the men with a deep pleasure for which they had no desire for words.

So that he would be home before the worst of the night cold, Garney Walch left an hour before dusk. Because both he and his ox were weary, he took the long way home through the forest, avoiding the hills of the morning. A quarter-mile down the right-hand fork of a muddy track that ran through to Ira Bye's sly grog shop, the ox stopped and refused to go on.

Raising his head from his memories and the sled, which he simply followed as though he were the dumb, obedient animal, Garney Walch's first impression was of how the bare feet splayed over the broken bracken fern seemed so small.

He stepped around the sled and the ox to get closer. The back of the body, ragged clothes partly torn away, was crawling with so many lice it more resembled an insect nest than a human being. Several bloody holes gored the exposed flesh where forest ravens had eaten, their unreadable footprints in the mud around. He dug the tip of his boot in under the shoulder and rolled the body out of the dirty puddle, and immediately felt ashamed for treating a fellow human being so.

He stood there silent. Mist was filling the forest and everything was lost in its soft white shroud. Beads of water ran down the white glistening trunks that stood like pillars of salt, rising, falling, crumbling. As his silver hair grew wet, as water began gathering like dew on his face, he felt increasingly lost in a dream.

For Garney Walch knew her. Only a few weeks before, he had seen her break into a drunken dance in the middle of a Hobart street before it was even noon—part native jig and something of a toff's dance, half-hyena and fully a princess, queer, lost, belonging and not belonging. A few had jeered, some threw scraps of food at her, urchins chased her as though she were a bird with broken wings.

It was not so hard to guess how she died—the twisted rag, the bruised neck, the torn dress—but he doubted there would be any trouble, far less an inquest.

His gaze followed the dead girl's open eyes upwards. Beyond, life went on as it always had, oblivious to tragedy or joy. Over the next ridge, in a rude, lonely cottage of boughs, a woman was moaning in childbirth, while down on the rocks a fisherman cursed after pulling up his pot only to discover the legs and shells of crayfish left by a thieving octopus.

'That's how it goes,' said Garney Walch softly, as he closed her eyes.

There was nothing left of her other than work. He picked her damp body up with hands that were at once very large and very gentle, and, placing it on the sled, he cleared the rags of bark away before laying her down, her head framed between his axe and saw.

She had been seven years old when he first swung her through the air and sat her on his cart and tweaked her toe. She had reminded him then of his dead daughter. She had been beautiful.

He tried to tally the passing years. The world was darkening, the long night was only beginning, a tree dropped a bough, a boobok owl ate a pardalote, and a black swan flew skyward. He dropped his head, his calculations done. She would have been seventeen years old.

'How it goes,' he murmured, 'and keeps on going.'

With the stringybarked back of a hand, the sawyer wiped a dead and milky eye, then stroked the ox on the muzzle and asked it to help him carry the poor child home, her dirty feet jolting over the sled's back as the ox took up its burden, their light-coloured soles disappearing into the longest night.